The Rock

I0742560

Maureen Mendelowitz

The Rock

The Rock
ISBN 978 1 76041 444 3
Copyright © text Maureen Mendelowitz 2017
Cover image: *Art in Glass* by Taryn Tollman

This is a work of fiction. Names, characters, events and incidents are the products of the author's imagination or used in a fictitious manner. Any resemblance to actual persons, living or dead, or actual events, is purely coincidental.

First published 2017 by
GINNINDERRA PRESS
PO Box 3461 Port Adelaide 5015
www.ginninderrapress.com.au

From Julian –

'This rock is more than a million years old. And in a million years it will still be here…'

'And us? Where will we be in a million years?'

'We'll be around. We may not be us. But we'll be around…'

'If not us, who will we be?'

'We may be birds. Or butterflies…'

'Will we know each other?'

'Yes. We'll always know each other…'

For Julian –

Always…

There is a rocky ledge that leans over the sea at Llandudno. It juts out on three sides, exposed to the changing shades of ocean and sky, the blues, the greys, the oranges and reds of sunset, and the pale violet hues of early dawn.

It is a hidden place. A steep flight of steps hewn from rock leads down from the road to a pristine crescent of white beach. At the far end, a wall of huge boulders are piled and lean haphazardly, one against the other.

The rock is beyond the boulders. It is comfortable, flat and smooth. Below is nothing but the wide ocean; above, the wide skies. The sunrise sometimes bathes it in crimson hues, and sometimes it is fiery in the red flames of sunset. But in the dark of night, its surface hardens in the glittering sparkle of stars and the moon etches its compact layers in a strong beam of white light.

The rock is difficult to find. There are only small spaces and narrow crevices to crawl through – a secret rock – hidden behind an ominous outcrop of huge boulders that signals the end of the beach and forbids anything beyond.

Daniel knew the rock.

How?

Did he find it as a small boy exploring? Did his mother call out, 'Daniel! Daniel! Where are you?' and run along that small crowded beach, and look out to the waves panic-stricken, and desperately ask, 'Have you seen my child? A small boy? With dark curly hair?' and sigh hugely and with great relief when that curly-headed boy, small and skinny, appeared from the outcrop and ran towards his mother shouting, 'Mama, I've found a rock! A big flat rock!' Did she scoop him up in her arms, crying and laughing and reprimanding, 'Daniel! Where were you? Don't ever do that again! I thought you were lost forever!' not listening to what he was saying, but smothering him with kisses?

Is that when Daniel found the rock?

Perhaps he found it as a boy wanting to escape the turmoil of his home. Did he run from the interminable arguments, the insults, and the vicious temper of his dad, jump on a bus, arrive at Llandudno, pace along the beach, and crawl through the crevices to hide away, to bury his head in his knees and cry, to scream into the wind, 'I hate him! I hate him! I wish he was dead!'

Or did he find it as a young man seeking solitude? Did he close his books in exhaustion and say, 'I've got to get out of here,' and leave the littered desk and medical tomes, and drive along that stretch of coast until he reached the little beach. Did he scramble though the crevices seeking to block out the smell of ether and sick bodies at the hospital, the lectures, the notes, the examinations, and wonder how much more he could take? Did he then come upon the flat wide rock, sit on its smooth surface, his back against a boulder and gaze out in wonder at the beauty and isolation of his find? Did he close his tired eyes and allow the songs of the sea and the soft breezes to envelop him and calm his crowded mind, to bring him quietude, to give him peace?

However it happened, it seemed to Maryssa that the rock belonged to him, a hidden secret place behind an inaccessible outcrop of boulders, a place that he had discovered, that only he would know.

It seemed as though it was also a porous rock, a rock that absorbed stains. There was no evidence of the drops of bright red blood on its smooth surface. The rock, the rain and the surf from the sea during high winds and severe storms, all had helped to remove it.

From the street the music could be heard, the beat, the rhythm. From the gate, voices, laughter.

The house was dimly lit, filtered with a rosy light from tiny bulbs strung across the ceiling of the lounge filled with images of people moving, people dancing.

Daniel and Ted walked up the path. Above them, the sky glittered and the moon hung, its glow touching the tops of trees whilst shrubs clustered darkly. The air was perfumed with frangipani. It was a warm and still evening but expectant, quietly waiting.

They'd spent the day swimming and playing tennis in the grounds of Ted's house, where Daniel stayed when he visited Johannesburg. Daniel prided himself on the peaceful hours he'd managed to spend with his friend, where he conscientiously avoided contentious issues – in particular, political discussions. From what he'd learned, Ted was heavily involved with the anti-apartheid movement at the university, giving talks and speeches. He'd long been aware of Ted's left-wing views but he now sensed an urgency and tension in his friend. Like a taut wire, Daniel thought. So they swam, and hit the ball on the court, and spoke of girls they fancied and guys they both knew.

'Blue Suede Shoes' created the beat as they walked into the crowded room filled with flushed faces, with smiles, with rhythm, with movement. As the song ended and before the next began, and before Maryssa realised it, Daniel had found his way to her, had his arm firmly around her, had taken her hand, had smiled down at her with his dark eyes.

Holding her, swaying to the music, he said, 'I'm Dan, Dan Simons, and you're Maryssa Klein.'

'How do you know?' She smiled at him, intrigued by his boldness.

'I asked one of the guys.'

She observed his darkly handsome face, his crisp dark hair. 'You're not from Jo'burg?' she asked.

'Cape Town.'

'Which part?'

'Sea Point.'

'Cape Town's a beautiful place.'

Something flickered within them, between them.

'What do you do?'

He smiled his thin smile. 'Medicine. I'm fourth year. And you?'

She saw his smile. 'I've just written matric.'

He'd noticed her immediately. Casting a glance around the room he'd seen her, her face, the sway of her hair, her straight shoulders. From a corner of the room, he'd observed her smile, her eyes, the light sliding from her cheekbones. He'd felt his senses quicken and asked, with a low whistle, 'Hey, Ted. Who is that?'

Ted followed his gaze. 'That's Maryssa. Maryssa Klein.' Turning to Daniel, he added protectively, 'A good friend of mine. Nice girl. Very nice girl…'

Daniel's gaze moved from her face to her narrow waist to the provocative sway of her hips. He waited for the song to end, moved through the crowd towards her and captured her in the curve of his arm. 'I'm Dan,' he'd said.

They danced and listened to each other's voices, his hand in the small of her back, her hand on his shoulder. He saw that her eyes were amber, that there were amber lights in her hair, that her hair was thick and lustrous, her lips soft and full, her smile soft, warm. He felt her breasts brush against his chest, her thighs touching his. He inhaled her perfume, light and flowery, and noted the softness of her hand in his.

She felt his height and the strength of his body. He leaned into her, commanded her, mastered her. He had a dark, clean, clinical feel about him, a sculptured lean feel. He was agile and alive. Electric.

They were set alight. In the rosiness of the room, closed in by the crowd, they were alone. Their senses were on fire. They could feel the beat of their hearts, their pulses beating. Their faces touched, their lips brushed, they looked deeply into each other's eyes.

'Come with me,' he said softly. He took her hand and led her into the garden, along a path, past the huddled bushes, the moon-brushed trees, to a hidden corner enclosed by a stone wall.

In that far corner of the garden, screened by the shrubs and trees, with the air perfumed and the sky burning with stars, they kissed, long and longingly. They held each other. They kissed again and again.

'I'm going home tomorrow,' he told her softly.

'Oh. Are you?' Her voice was filled with disappointment.

'I am. I have to be at the hospital on Monday. But,' he held her face in both hands and looked at her intently, 'we'll see each other again… Of that I'm absolutely sure…'

It was a huge house, square and squat in a large flat garden. It was a flat-looking house. Closed off. Unlived in.

'Why doesn't your gardener plant any flowers?' As was Ted's response to all questions he did not want to answer, he simply said nothing.

Inside, large rooms filled with huge couches and cabinets, and a dining room table large enough for twenty seated guests, led from a narrow gloomy passage. Heavy velvet drapes kept out the sun and the air was stale. At the end of the passage was a sterile cavernous kitchen.

The study, with floor-to-ceiling bookshelves and a movable ladder fixed to a rail, was lit up by a large block of unfettered sunlight.

Maryssa wandered into the room. 'Teddy! Wow!' She ran her fingers across the spines, read some of the titles. 'What a fantastic collection! Do you ever read any of these?'

They climbed the wide curved staircase to the first floor, to the photographic studio. The space was bright and alive with photographic equipment, with portfolios and photographs stacked along the walls. Blown-up images of a lioness with her cubs, a curled cobra, an eagle with spread wings hung from frames. This was Ted's father's work. Maryssa stood in front of a tram somewhere in Europe that seemed to be moving towards her. It must have been taken within inches of being run over by the tram. She could almost hear the driver tooting his horn and hysterically gesticulating for the mad photographer to clear out of the way. It had won first prize, said a newspaper cutting stuck to its frame.

The nude shots were hidden in a cupboard. As a child, Ted had come across them by chance. He was both intrigued and embarrassed by them, not understanding the pleasurable uncomfortable feelings they'd aroused in him.

There were no family shots, no proud pictures of Ted as a baby, no proud parents showing off their only child. There was nothing of a young wife, a smiling young mother, a young and happy family.

'Because there was no family. There was no mother. She disappeared when I was a few months old. Ran off with the captain of a ship. Believe it or not, that's what she did. She met him when they were on some cruise. They fell for each other and she packed her bags and left to be with him…'

'Where's she now?'

'Dead. Apparently, she died a while ago. She wasn't Jewish. Got converted through the Reform Shul. One of those quick meaningless jobs. My dad said she drank like a fish, smoked incessantly and hardly ate. He wasn't surprised to hear that she didn't last long…'

'You never knew her?'

'Never. There was a photograph of her that I once saw. But that's my only recollection of her. I was five months old when she left. Dinah brought me up. She used to tie me to her back and do the housework and the cooking and whatever else. When I was older, she'd walk me to school and fetch me in the afternoons…'

'Was she like a mother to you?'

'A mother? I wouldn't know. I don't know what a mother is. What's a mother, Shmoe? You have one. Tell me, what is a mother?'

'A mother? Well. I can only tell you about my mother. Um… Where do I start? Well, for one thing, my mother's the kindest person I've ever known. She'll do anything she can for me, for all of us. She helps me whenever I need her. She works, but she's always at the end of a telephone, always available to me in every way. It's hard to describe really. I suppose the best way of putting it is that she's always there, no matter what. And she loves us. That's what it is. She really loves us. She looks at us with such love in her eyes.'

'From what you tell me – and it all sounds right – I didn't have a mother. I had a nanny, a competent responsible nanny, who saw to my needs. Did she love me? No, she did not. Not to say that she was unkind. There were times when she was very good to me. Very comforting. But, in reality, she was doing a job. That's all. Then there were times when she was angry, moody, when she wouldn't answer me if I spoke to her. Not turn round. Have her back to me, and I'd get very cut up and lock myself in my room. But, to tell the truth, she was the only real person in my life and over the years I got to know her, to understand her, to tolerate her black moods, to recognise her frustrations, her repressed anger, her unfulfilled needs. And, amazingly, she's still with us today, cooking, cleaning and hanging the washing…'

'And your dad?'

'He's OK. He tried. But he was away a lot. Always brought me fancy presents. Thought the gifts would make up for not being around. Make up for the loneliness, the sadness that always seemed to be with me as a kid. He used to bring me expensive clothes – a leather jacket or a pair of imported shoes. But what does that mean? Nothing. To me, those things meant absolutely nothing…' He turned away from her, lit a cigarette and stared out of the window.

Smoke drifted. A shaft of sunlight fell diagonally across him. The room was silent.

Then he turned to her and said brightly and with the trace of a smile, 'Hey! Shmoe! Enough of all this gloom and doom… It's all in the far-distant past. Come on! Let's take some photos of you. Here. Wear this.' He tossed a giant sombrero to her and flashed the camera as she put it on the back of her head.

'Wait, Ted. I wasn't ready…'

'And put these on.' Giant gold hoop earrings.

'Where does all this come from?'

'My dad. He uses this stuff.'

He took a candid shot of her as she drank from a glass of milk. 'You look like a milkmaid!' he grinned.

'And you,' she shrieked, tipping some of the milk over him, 'you look like a leaking milk bottle!'

Milk dripped from the end of his nose. They laughed hysterically.

Then Ted stopped laughing. He looked at Maryssa and said, 'You're pretty, you know…' then, pausing, added, 'sometimes.' and ducked as she aimed to throw the rest of the milk at him.

'What about your dad? How's it going with him?' Ted squinted at her through the haze of cigarette smoke.

'Not good. I'm in a state every time someone comes to take me out.'

'I can imagine. It can't be easy living with that. Not for any of you.'

'No. It's really difficult. I don't discuss it with anyone because I really hope that people don't know about it. But I'm sure that word gets around. I just hope that they don't judge me because he drinks. You know what I mean.'

She sat cross-legged on the carpet, her hands clasped. All traces of her smile were gone. 'Did I tell you what happened on the night of my matric dance? I invited Justin to come with me.'

There are only a few years between being a girl and becoming a woman — a few years between thirteen and seventeen. Between hiding breasts and showing the crease between them. There are only a few years between flatties and high heels. Between giggles and slow smiles. Between hating walking past a crowd of boys and loving it.

There are these few years to learn the rules. What will please and what will cause others to look down their noses at you. How to be responsible for what you say and how you say it. How to play the game.

Because it is a game.

In Johannesburg, city of gold, city of glitter, city of rapid turnover, you need to know the rules. It's a quicksilver place with neat twists of the tongue, the right inclination of the head, the proper set of shoulders.

It's money of course. It's the city where money talks. Sometimes you can slip between the cracks and mix where it counts. If you've got the right look. If you get lucky…

But no matter how well you play the game, there are instances when, no matter how you look, how you act, you will not win.

No matter how much you are shown off — no matter how often you are driven around in open sports cars to the Bai Taberin or to Ciro's — you have to remember one thing: when it comes to tachlis, *when you have to be seriously considered, when you are being rated in the marriage stakes, you are measured differently. For in Johannesburg, every Jew knows. Who's got money. Who's successful. Who's got the respect.*

And those who are ordinary.

If you fit into any of those categories, you should be OK. Even in the ordinary category.

But if you're like me — if your dad's a drunk — then the dice are irretrievably loaded against you. Even though I'm known to be one of the most popular girls in Jo'burg.

Because the guys that I want – the desired category guys – they are not allowed to choose me. That can't happen. Not in happy Tinsel Town. You see, just under the glamour, the fun, the camaraderie, is a tough set of rules. Headed by the word yichis. Yichis *means choose right. The parents know. The mothers see to it. They're there to help their sons to choose right. They won't let you break the rules. They won't let you get above yourself. They won't allow you to cause their sons any upsets.*

Because in this town, everybody knows. Everybody talks. Everybody sits in judgement.

In this town, you live by the rules.

Justin, Ted knew, was her first love, her first passion. She adored him. She'd go anywhere with him. Just wanted to be with him. She'd sit quietly for hours in the laboratory just to be in his company.

Justin. Third-year psychology. Doing a paper on some aspect of behaviour of rats under specified circumstances. Justin – tall between the cages. Observing. Absorbed. She watched him taking notes, his dark hair curling in the back of his neck. Behind his horn-rimmed glasses, distracted and haggard under white lights, he pushed his long fingers through his hair. It needs cutting, she thought. But Justin was unconcerned about how he looked, vague about most things except for his work, his rats. Then his focus was as sharp as rats' claws.

In the stillness of the silent laboratory, she watched him and daydreamed.

When he knocks on the door, I'll be standing there in misty light in a swirl of peach organza with soft music in the background.

She'll keep the lounge in darkness to hide the shabby couch, the faded curtains, the old carpet.

I'll play soft music…

Her mother, sensing her excitement, sends her to Putzy's. Charles will make her dress. He carefully chooses the fabric to enhance the colour of her eyes, to bring a touch of peach to her pale cheeks. Maryssa looks as lovely as she dreamt she would. Her eyes glow, her hair, a mass of auburn waves frames her flushed and pretty face.

When the doorbell rings, she is alight with excitement. Her father is in the bedroom. Her sisters have been warned not to peek or giggle.

'It has to be perfect,' she tells them.

The lounge is in darkness. Music filters softly. With heart beating fast, she opens the door.

But it isn't Justin. Oh God. It isn't him. She stares in disbelief, in stunned silence.

'Hello, Maureen,' she hears in broad Irish brogue. In Bob and Aileen Wilson brogue. They stand in the doorway with whiskied breath, smiling broadly, behind them their broad son Rory.

'Oh no,' Maryssa groans.

'Doncha look grund, yung wimmin. Just grund. Yer goin' out, urr ye?'

The bedroom door opens. Her mother's head appears. Her sisters peep from the end of the passage.

'What's going on?' Her father's voice comes from the room.

'It's Bob,' says her mother in despair. 'Bob and Aileen…'

'Bob!' Her father calls out, holding up his trousers. 'Come in! Come in!' Excited and delighted, forgetting his false teeth, he rolls down the passage switching on all the lights.

'Err we introodin' then?' asks Aileen.

'No, no! Of course not! Happy to see you!' He's forgotten his promises to Maryssa. He's forgotten her matric dance evening. It's his evening now. A joyful turn of events. Bob's here! His office friend. His drinking friend.

The lights are on! The music's off! The whisky's out! The whisky goblets, the ice bucket…

Maryssa's eyes fill with tears of frustration. 'Oh God, my mascara…' she cries and runs to the bathroom.

That's when Justin rings the doorbell and her father answers, holding up his trousers, a glass in his hand.

'Allo, Allo, Allo! Come in!' he grins toothlessly. 'I'm Maryssa's father. Sorry about my teeth. I lent them to my brother. He had to go to a wedding. Meet my friend Bob…'

Bob roars with approval at Ellis's joke, stumbles to his feet and bumbles, 'Hudja doo,' shaking Justin's hand long and hard whilst peering at him with red-rimmed whiskied eyes.

Through a buzzing sound in her ears, Maryssa hears her father say importantly 'Off you go then. Have a good time, and don't you bring her home late. Don't bring my beautiful daughter home late.'

Ted sat opposite her on the floor leaning against the wall. He blew smoke rings, then said, 'That's not good.'

'I know. I was so embarrassed I wanted to DIE!'

'I can imagine.'

'I mean… The whole evening was spoilt for me. I kept thinking about it.'

'How was he?'

'He was very nice. He never seemed to notice.'

'Justin? I'm sure he noticed. He's sharp. He'd have picked up on everything.'

'Well, he never said anything. Never made me feel bad.'

'He wouldn't have made you feel bad. He's a really well-bred guy. Comes from a very classy family. But his mother's a helluva snob. Have you seen him since then?'

'No, I haven't heard from him.'

'You probably won't.'

'Well, that's what I mean. That's what I'm talking about. I'm telling you, Ted. I'll never marry any of the guys I'd want. No one decent will go for me. Not with a father like him.' Her eyes filled with pain as she softly said, 'My dad will always spoil my chances.'

In the stillness of the afternoon, they became silent. Ted stretched out on the carpet, his head in Maryssa's lap, his eyes closed. Maryssa glanced down the length of him. From that angle, he looked thinner, elongated, and his feet, toes turned towards the ceiling, looked longer than they were.

She leaned her back and the back of her head against the wall and watched the big block of sunlight move imperceptibly across the room. She saw the dust motes dancing. She thought of her dad.

She remembered how particular he was about his clothes and all his things – his shoe brush, his silver shoe horn, his hat brush, all in their allotted places in his wardrobe. She recalled how he buffed his shoes until they shone, how, each morning, he brushed his brown felt hat.

She remembered his stories. The time he stood on a box in a big shop window in the centre of town advertising the great new sensation – Black Jack Chewing Gum. Hundreds of people watched as he chewed the gum and blew gigantic bubbles. At the end of the afternoon, he had an aching jaw and black gum that stuck to the tip of his nose, his hair, his ears. But he skipped home, happy, with packets of gum in his pockets for his brothers and sisters and half a crown for his efforts.

She remembered the story of the Best Legs Competition that was held at the local bioscope. The curtain came down halfway on the stage so that only the competitors' legs could be seen. When the winner was announced, it was her dad's sister Hester who won first prize. The crowd roared with approval. Then the curtain was rolled up. The audience saw Hester's face, her large nose and her small dark close-together eyes. They were quiet for a moment, then the booing began. Hester fled the stage in tears and stayed in her room for a week.

'That's what turned her nasty,' her mother would say.

As the light began to fade, Maryssa remembered the story of Solly Tannenbaum.

On most nights, Ellis stumbles off the tram, lurches past the bakery, the barber's and the dry cleaners, with his brown hat pushed to the back of his head. This hat that is meticulously brushed each morning and angled smartly over one eye changes position in the uneven evenings, loses its chic as the pavements rise uneasily to meet him.

When he's sober, his drinking habit disturbs him, but, try as he might, the pull is too strong. 'A couple of drinks never does any harm,' he thinks. He comforts himself by saying, 'One thing's for sure. You'll never catch me drunk on the job.' 'Never missed a day's work,' is another thing he often says.

On good nights, when they were children, they'd curl up on the couch in their candlewick dressing gowns. He told them stories about his family, about his mother and father who came from Russia to England. To the East End. He proudly told them about his dad, who was a bespoke tailor. Maryssa used to repeat to herself, 'Bespoke tailor from the East End'. It sounded important. He'd died when Ellis was two years old. 'Never knew him,' he said gruffly.

He also spoke about the language of the Cockneys, referring to his feet as his 'plates', to his mouth as his 'north and south'.

From the newspaper he read 'Dagwood' and 'Curly Wee' to them, his lips smacking, his finger pointing to the pictures in the comic strips as they leaned over his arms and shoulders.

He loves them. They're his daughters. They're his Three Smart Girls.

Even when he's drunk, when he disturbs and destroys, she doesn't hate him. She may cry. She may cover her head with her pillow. She may be filled with feelings of helplessness and hurt.

But despite all, Maryssa loves him.

He's her dad.

He comes from the Apollo Cafe with a jug foaming with ginger beer and ice cream.

'Tell us the story of Solly Tannenbaum!'

'Solly Tannenbaum? Again?'

'Yes, Dad. Please. Tell us.'

'Well, there was this boy Solly Tannenbaum. He lived round the corner from us.'

'And he never had a father,' we chime.

'No. His father was dead.' He paused. 'Like mine.'

We sit quietly. Waiting.

'Anyway, Solly was small for his age. Very thin. And every day there was this bully Thomas Breytenbach. Waiting for him.'

'And then? What happened then?'

'He used to spit at Solly. Or trip him. Or punch him. Solly tried to go another way but Thomas always found him. Every day, Solly came to school crying but we didn' know that all this was going on. He never told us. Then one day he didn' come to school at all. I went to see him in the afternoon an' he was in his room. "Solly," I said, "are you sick?" "No," he says. Then he says, "Jus' leave me alone! Go away!" "Why din' you come to school?" I ask him. "I don' have to tell you!" he says.'

Ellis pauses. He lights a cigarette.

'Then what happened, Dad?'

'Then I say to him, "Solly," I say, "you have to tell me. I know something's going on. I know something's wrong."'

'Then?' We wait.

'Then he starts to cry. Like a baby. I say to him, "What's it, Solly? Tell me." Then he tells me. He tells me that every day Thomas waits for him. Spits on him. Punches him. Trips him up. But then Solly din' come to school. Thomas had done something else. He stood on the corner as Solly walks by and he laughs. Then he says to Solly, "Hey, Solly. You dirty little Jew. You filthy little Kike with the cut-off pippee…"'

My mother catches his eye. She shakes her head.

'So then…'

'So then I said, "Is that what happened?" An' I said to Solly, "Don' worry."

'And Solly says, "What d'ya mean?" An' I say 'Don' you worry Sol. I'll see to this," An' Solly says, an' he was scared, real scared. Solly says, "Watcha gonna do?" An' I tell him, "Don' you worry Sol. Leave it with me. An' I go off and look for Thomas.'

Ellis leans his head into the sofa. We lean forward. We know this story.

'Then.' he says. 'I look for Thomas. I find him. At the Greek. Eating chips. "Thomas," I say.

'He looks at me.

"Hey, Thomas."

"Whaddja want?" he asks.

"Come here," I say. "I want to ask you something."

"What?" he asks.

"Come outside," I tell him.

'He comes out. He's got a big grin on his face.

"What?" he says.

"I wanna ask you. Did you call Solly a dirty Jew?"

"An' what if I did?" he says. "Waddja gain' to do about it?"'

'Then?' we say. 'Then what happened?'

'Then I see red. I smack the chips out of his hands. They're all over the street. Then I lay into him. I punch him so hard that the Greek comes out of the shop and pulls me off him. His nose is bleeding and his eyes are black and blue an' I'm banging his head on the pavement.'

'Then?'

'Then I go back to Solly. "Sol," I say. "I've fixed it. He won' bother you again. Remember Sol," I tell him. "Remember. From now on you got nothing to worry about." An' that was the end of it. Never bothered him again.'

This is the story Maryssa likes to hear over and again.

This is the story where she comes to know her dad as brave and fearless and loyal.

This is the other side of her dad…

It was Maryssa's last year in school, and, as was the custom, her headmistress met with her and Betty to discuss her future.

'She's a clever girl. She should go to university.' Miss Ramsey's grey hair was piled onto her head, held with pins. She wore a grey buttoned suit and sat in her grey office where even the sun's rays faded.

Betty sat upright, her knees together. She listened and nodded. Maryssa's eyes strayed to the window, to the branch of an old oak, knobbled and grey.

'University?' the chorus of aunts exclaimed.

'Her? Ridiculous!'

'Better she finds a nice boy. Settles down. Gets married. Has a family.'

'Exactly. She needs a good boy. A *mensch*. Someone who earns a good living.'

'That's right. If she finds the right person, she can live in a nice house, drive a nice car, have nice friends...'

'And kids.'

'What about Betty and Ellis? She should try to help them.'

'Give them some pleasure, some *nachas*.'

'That's right. That's what life's about. Not some useless university course.'

'Some useless BA.'

'What's that?'

'Bachelor of Arts, I think.'

'Bachelor of Arts? Bugger all, I think. BA – Bugger All!'

But Maryssa enquires anyway. 'Can you please give me some information about the logopaedics course?'

It's a Bachelor of Science degree and a year postgraduate. Four years. Four years of fees. Four years of not earning money. They're right of course. University's not for her. She swallows her disappointment and signs up for a secretarial course.

'Shorthand typing,' says her dad. 'Best thing for a girl.'

Ted drove her to the interview and waited for her.

'Thanks, Ted.'

'How did it go? Who did you see?'

'The head of the Pathology department. Professor Stern. He asked me if I'd ever seen a dead body.'

'Don't tell me the job means dead bodies.'

'It does. I have to attend post-mortems and take notes. He asked me how I felt about that.'

'What did you say?'

'I said, "Fine!" I said, "Dead bodies don't worry me at all!"' She shuddered.

'So…' Ted drew hard on his cigarette. 'You told them what they wanted to hear?'

'Of course. I want the job.'

'But how do you know how you'll feel? I mean, you won't just see dead bodies. You'll probably have to watch them being cut up. That's what they do in pathology. Cut them up, examine them for disease, for the cause of death. How do you feel about that?'

'I'll deal with it. I'll get used to it.'

'You don't have to. You don't have to subject yourself to that, Shmoe. There are other jobs.'

'I know. But I've been offered this one. I can't mess around. I have to start work. As soon as possible. I have to see to myself and try to help my mother. You know that. And one job is much like another. That's what my mom says. And you can get used to anything. She says that too.'

'I still say that sitting in a mortuary with a crowd of students watching them carve up a cadaver must be the absolute bottom of the pile.'

'I told you, I'll be OK. I can switch off. I can block out. I've been doing that my whole life.'

'That's where you and I differ, Shmoe. I can't do that. I see things exactly as they are. And, at times, well, it's very painful.'

'But Ted, don't you find the need to protect yourself, to put up barriers?'

'I can't do that. I've tried but that hurts more than the pain I feel when something gets to me. I prefer to go through the agony of it. Trouble is, I don't always get through it too well. Sometimes I don't get through it at all.'

Yesterday, he told her, he'd learned that his neighbour's maid's baby was no longer with her. 'I'd see her sitting on the pavement with him. Feeding him. He was such a sweet little kid.'

'But they always send their kids home, Ted. That's what happens.'

'No! That's NOT what happens!' His voice was raised. 'That's the way we've made it happen. It's OK for white kids to be with their mothers. But not for the native kids. They've got to go back to the kraal. Or run around the locations looked after by sick old grandmothers. Or disinterested strangers. They get sick. They die. But they're natives, so who cares? Nobody. Nobody gives a continental shit!'

Ted said something else. 'The worst thing for me is that this woman accepts the separation from her kid without an argument. She seemed fine this morning when I saw her. She wasn't upset. One day she's breast feeding a six-month-old baby, the next day the baby's gone and it doesn't seem to bother her.'

He lights another cigarette. 'Christ, man! Just like an animal. Just like a fucking animal.'

He turned to Maryssa with an intense look. 'That's what we've done,' he said slowly, deliberately. 'We've turned them into fucking animals.'

She sits on the late afternoon tram and stares out of the window unaware of the glare of the setting sun. 'I saw a dead body today,' she says silently to herself. Glancing at the people standing in the aisle, at their flattened expressions, she thinks, 'Today I saw a diseased body. I smelled a body that gave off the smell of the dead. I heard the scalp being ripped off. I saw it being pulled down over a dead face. I heard the sound of a saw zigzagging through the skull. I saw the brain come out like an encapsulated jelly. None of these people will ever see what I saw today. A dead body being sliced up.'

On a warm and sunny Sunday, the friends drive in Ted's open truck to the mountains in Magaliesberg. The suspension in the vehicle is bad and they're jolted with every bump in the road. A big bottle of Coke is passed from mouth to mouth, and, hanging grimly on to the sides, they accompany each jerk with joyous yells and groans and loud laughter. Someone sings and the others join in, ignoring Ted's loud, 'For God's sake! Shut the hell up!' from the driver's seat.

'Hey, Ted! I'm starving! Let's stop for hot dogs,' shouts Clive against the protesting creaks of the truck.

'You're always starving! Wait for the bully beef,' yells Ted.

With closed eyes, Maryssa faces the wind and feels the sun on her face. Her hair blows into a bright tangled mass. On either side of the road is the country, with cows grazing, a grove of fruit trees, the earthy smell of tilled fields. There are far horizons, hills that blend into the sky, the loud call of an unseen bird. She feels light and free, as free as the bird that calls, as free as the whisper of a distant cloud.

On a dusty road they stop at an *algemener handelaar*, a general store whose motto says, 'Everything from a Needle to an Anchor' on a cracked and peeling board above the door. Pushing past a curtain made of threaded beads they find, to their amazement, that the owner has fresh Vienna sausages and soft white rolls. They wait for their hot dogs and, in the close spicy air of the shop, they're surrounded by shelves packed with tea and sugar and rice, with tinned food, paraffin lamps and stoves, cooking pots and tightly rolled blankets.

Back on the truck, Maryssa eats her sausage that's bursting out of its skin and ribboned with mustard and gives her roll to Clive, whose stomach jiggles with each bump on the road. They jostle against each other, these friends, slap each other on the back, smile and joke and laugh, and Maryssa feels happy and secure. Also, Ted's at the helm. She feels safe with Ted. He knows what he's doing. He knows where he's going.

The mountains are silent.

At a farmer's shed on the lowlands, they mount sad-looking sagging horses who slowly climb up paths strewn with ancient pebbles and cross shallow streams that disappear into the grey flat plains. There's a constant buzz of insects and the sun breaking through the thorn trees becomes moving pebbles of light.

Ted rides ahead. He's been here before. He wants to show them what he found.

An hour passes. The heat beats down and sweat trickles down their backs. Irritated, they wipe their faces and say, 'Jesus! It's bladdy hot,' and 'How much further?' and 'Jeez, Ted! Are you sure you know where you're going?'

Ted's hair falls across his forehead and he glances back but does not answer.

The horses climb through rocky clefts where there is no protection from the sun. The animals' sweat mingles with the perspiration of the group. Their faces are flushed, their hair plastered, they're exhausted and frustrated. They take no comfort in Ted's reassurance that they are nearly at their destination.

He turns around, looks at them and says 'God! Look at you. You are a sorry lot.'

The climb levels into a plateau of brown grass and flat rocks.

'That's where we're going. Over there. Just tie your horses to a tree. We'll get them water.'

'We'll get *us* water,' mutters Clive under his breath.

'This is it. This is what I want to show you.'

They trudge up a small path and come to a large pool of water surrounded by rocky outcrops. The friends are silent. They stare at the almost perfect circle, dark and impenetrable, its black surface still and smooth except for ripples from a low waterfall at one end.

'This is amazing.'

'Wow!'

'Is it safe to swim?'

'Sure, it's safe. Safe as houses.' Ted strips down to briefs and dives in.

The water is so cold that it takes Maryssa's breath away. She moves her arms rapidly and kicks her feet, treads water and gasps for air, then hauls herself onto a warm flat shelf of rock, and stretches onto her back, shivering. 'It's freezing!'

'But amazing.' Ted sits, leaning on thin knees, his hair plastered, squinting against the sun.

With eyes closed, Maryssa lies silent, absorbing the warmth from the rock, the stillness and the perfect peace of the place. There is something else too, something she can't define.

'You've felt it?' He watches her.

'I have.'

'I knew you would. I don't know about the others, but I knew you would get it, Shmoe.'

'There's something here. Something extraordinary,' she says softly. 'Something I'd like to put in a bottle, seal and take home with me – something ecstatic – an ecstasy moment…'

'There is. Capture as much of it as you can. Moments like this are as rare as blue diamonds…'

'Come on, guys. Let's eat.'

'I'm starving!'

'Bring on the food!'

'Open the bully beef!'

Ted watches them. His pale eyes narrow and he blows one smoke ring through another. 'You're all meat and potatoes, man,' he tells his friends.

'Meat and potatoes? What's wrong with that?' demands Jeff. 'I'm not like you. I live in the real world. The world as it is.' He swallows a tinned peach and licks the juice from his fingers.

'I don't think you do. You think you do, but I think you guys are like Plato's prisoners.'

'Who? Christ! Here he goes again. Pleeeze! Don't go quoting one of your ancient philosophers.'

'What prisoners?' Maryssa asks quickly.

'Plato talks about these prisoners.' Ted stares ahead. His voice is quiet. 'They were chained to the wall of a cave. Even their heads were anchored so that they could only look forward. Behind them was a fire. Between their backs and the fire was a road. All these guys could see were the shadows of people walking along the road, shadows that flickered on the wall in front of them.'

'Ah man, what's the point?'

'The point is – they believed the shadows to be the real thing. You see, they never knew better. They'd never seen real people. They only saw shadows. Then, one day, one of the prisoners breaks free. He wanders into the sunlight and he's nearly blinded by its brightness. He can hardly look into the flames. But slowly he becomes used to it. He sees people for the first time. He begins to realise how unsubstantial, how thin on the ground, his former life has been.'

'And then?'

'Then he's taken back into the cave, back to being a prisoner again. But now he cannot distinguish the shadows on the wall because…' Ted turns to look at them, 'he's seen the real world. His buddies continue to be content with the shadows. They probably wouldn't have left the cave, even if they could.' He yawns. 'That's how most people are, boys, living in their little worlds, looking at images, accepting the shadows. Out of touch. Completely out of touch.' He yawns again, lights another cigarette, stretches out and pulls a cap over his eyes.

Ted, her sensitive friend, who seeks out secret places, quiet places, places of water, of insects and birds, drives off the road between the black trees. Moonbeams fracture on the surface of the river and smooth white pebbles glow like giant pearls. The sky, blacker than the trees, is pierced with a thousand stars – the Belt of Orion, the Dog, the Three Sisters, and the lonely and majestic Evening Star.

The stream plays music. A frog croaks.

They are warm in the comfort of it. Cosseted in the black and white of it. Ted's arm cushions Maryssa's head. He kisses her and his kiss tastes of cigarettes and mints.

That is all. A soft kiss in a dark glen. They lie together in this cupped place of stillness and solitude.

Until he sits up. His profile is sharp in a searching shaft of moonlight. He unscrews his pen, chews its end, spits out bits of it, and writes on the back of her cigarette box.

Then he says with immense sadness, 'I'm beginning to realise it Shmoe, beginning to see the hopelessness of it,' and gives her the box.

She reads:

> There is no grey
> White and black
> Hounds tooth or stripe
> Spotted or check
> Or stars in the night
> The two do not flow
> They face each other,
> Each fighting for space
>
> BLACK & WHITE
> ARE EACH TOO STRONG
> THEY SEE EACH OTHER
> BUT WILL NOT GET ALONG

Then he mutters, 'It's not working.'

In the dark shadows, he turns to her and says, 'Sometimes you just have to walk away. You try. God, you try, but it just doesn't seem to work.' His face is filled with anguish. 'It's tearing the guts out of me.'

He looks away and skims a pebble across the water breaking the moon's white path. Softly he says, more to himself than to her,

'Sometimes you have no choice. Sometimes you just have to walk away.' He draws deeply on a cigarette, withdrawing from her into the solemn darkness of himself.

Their drive home is dark and silent.

'Are you coming, Shmoe?'

'No, Ted. I'm not. My dad had a fit when he heard that I was at that last meeting. He says the secret police are at those meetings and he doesn't want me near them.'

'How would he know that? Hundreds of people come. They're not worried. The hall's packed.'

'Well, I won't be there. He's adamant. He says it's dangerous. They take names. They put you on the blacklist. People are fleeing the country. Some disappear… They're never heard from again.'

'Look, Shmoe, this is Varsity. If we can't have a forum on campus, then we're in big trouble. There must be some place where we can talk about justice. You know what's going on, how unfair everything is. If we don't stand up for what we believe in, if we don't talk about the inequities of this damned apartheid system, the country will go one way – down. It'll get worse and worse.'

'I know all that. But I'm not coming. It scares me. The whole thing terrifies me. And let me tell you, you'd better be careful yourself. You know you're being watched. You could end up in big trouble.'

'I'm not worried. I need to say what I feel. I can't accept this. I can't live like an ostrich. If you want to bury your head in the sand, that's your business. Although, I must say, I credited you with more than that. You talk about the injustices, you make all the right noises, but when push comes to shove you run away.'

'Don't talk to me like that. To tell you the truth, I don't know where I stand. I don't know what to say. I was born into this.'

'Into what?'

'A native girl who cooks in the kitchen, a native boy who cleans the floor and brushes the lavatory…'

'That he can't use, even if he's bursting to go. As if his piss is any different to mine.'

'They've got their lavatories.'

'Up three flights of stairs.'

'Oh God, they're doing a job… I don't want to look further than that.'

'Exactly. You're satisfied with knowing nothing about them. Just as long as your food gets cooked and your lavatory gets cleaned. You don't even know their surnames, John or Sixpence, or maybe Schneider, named after some guy who gave his mother ten shillings a month for thirty years until she dropped dead.'

'Look, I'm leaving. I don't have to listen to this. As I said, this is what I was born into – separate toilets, separate entrances, separate queues. Separate lives. It's wrong but this is what I know.' She picks up her bag and impatiently brushes the away the tears that well up in her eyes. 'You make me mad. You really do!'

Ted watches the back of her as she walks away. From his thin cheeks, a blue smoke ring puffs and passes through another that is already blurring, already dispersing.

Ted's hands emphasise his words. He moves away from the lectern. His voice is strained, his eyes intense. 'Don't you see? The whole Western world is ruled by economics, by capitalists wanting to make money – the more the better. They don't care who gets trampled on in the process. In every country where money is God, the people are alienated, divided into the haves and the have nots. The only way the poor people, those who are being trampled on, have any way of liberating themselves, is through force. Think about it. The natives here are just another commodity. If the money makers need more labourers, they simply ship them in from the Transkei or from some other godforsaken place, on contract. Then they're shipped back like pieces of furniture. No thought goes into their needs – their wives, their kids, their communities. And when they're not needed, when there's a slump in business, no one, but no one in the whole fucking system cares what happens to them.

'The capitalists know that this commodity will never run out. There are millions of natives all clamouring for jobs. And while we're talking about their jobs, let's talk about their salaries. What they get paid. Jesus! Just enough to keep them alive so that they can go out and do solid sweat and toil. I mean, where would all the rich buggers be without this cheap labour? They make fortunes because of all these poor guys who have to grovel for work. From the profits, the whites acquire more businesses, build more factories. Then, with their conglomerates, they also put out the small businesses, the little guys who try to make a go on their own.

'Another thing,' Ted rushes on, his hair hanging over his forehead, 'There's no satisfaction for the labourers in the work they do – no job satisfaction. No requirements for initiative. They do as they're told. They work all day, all week, all year on something that doesn't belong to them and never will. They don't use their minds. They work automatically. Humanity is lost in the takeover of commerce and industry.

'I tell you people, all this work is what Marx called "the activity under the domination, coercion and yolk of another man". That man is the bossman. He's alien. He's hostile. There's no brotherly love there. There's no trust. It's all bargaining and exchanging needs. They stop seeing each other as human beings.'

'What about a minimum wage structure?' calls out someone in the audience.

'That doesn't solve anything. That becomes "nothing better than a slave salary". The worker remains the same – insignificant, with no dignity. The only way to go, as Marx says, is to abolish wages and alienated labour and the ownership of property.'

Ted tells them, 'The words of Feuerbach are engraved on Marx's tombstone. They read as follows: "The philosophers have only interpreted the world in various ways: the point is, to change it."

'This doesn't mean that philosophy isn't important. It doesn't mean that revolution is all that matters. But Marx says that we'll never solve the problems of philosophy by a passive interpretation of the world as it is. We need to change the world to resolve the philosophical contradictions that are inherent in it.

'Show the workers what role they need to play by quoting what other suppressed workers have done throughout history. Show them how capitalism continues to take them for a ride. Wake them up. Make them aware of the tremendous power they wield. Teach them the word Revolution! Teach them how to use their strength. Teach them when to strike.

'For God's sake! Wake them up!'

Dennis Sobukwe stands unsure, hesitates, then knocks softly on Maryssa's door. His thin frame is swathed in a patched white coat, his stethoscope jammed into his pocket. 'Sorry to disturb Mizz Klein...' The fifth year medical student's voice is apologetic.

'It's OK, Dennis. I'm not that busy. What can I do for you?'

'It's this book, Mizz Klein. I loan it from Steven Sher. It's too much money for me to buy. I wanted to ask Mizz Klein if you can please type the first three chapters for me. We have a test on Monday and I need these notes.' His voice rushes on. 'I know it's a lot but I can pay you. Of course, I will pay you.'

'Let's have a look. The first three chapters. It is quite a lot of typing but I think I'll manage it. I type quite fast. You'll have to give me a couple of days.'

'That's OK, mizz. I can learn fast.'

'OK. I've also got a typewriter at home. What I can't fit in here I'll do there. Tell you what, why don't you come to my flat tomorrow evening and pick them up then?'

'That would be very fine, Mizz Klein. I finish my ward round and can come to you about seven o'clock. I have my bike.'

'They'll be ready. This is my address...' Then Maryssa looks up from the book and says, 'Dennis, I hope you don't mind me saying this, but your eyes look very strained. I mean, they're so red and puffy. You should see to them. Go to an optometrist. You may need reading glasses.'

'I know, mizz. It's not from my eyes. It's from the candle. It flickers and gives off smoke. We got no electricity in Sophiatown.'

'Do you mean you're studying by candlelight?'

'Yes. It's the only light I have.'

'That's terrible. It must be very hard for you...'

Dennis shrugs. He does not answer.

Maryssa had seen him sitting on the steps of medical school each day at lunchtime eating sandwiches. He was always in the same spot against the wall, always on his own. She felt his aloneness, and, when their eyes met, she would greet him and ask how he was.

She thought how admirable he was, studying medicine by candlelight, riding a bicycle the long distances to and from the native location to medical school each day. She thought how difficult his life was compared to the other students.

'Quite remarkable. He's really quite amazing,' she says aloud to herself.

When the doorbell rang the following evening, Maryssa was on the phone. She gave no thought to Dennis as she chatted with a friend about a blind date she'd been on that had gone horribly wrong. They laughed hysterically as she described the date's large ears. 'His reflection through the glass door looked as though he had three heads! And…' she almost collapsed with laughter. 'Listen to this…he keeps safety pins on the inside of his jacket lapel. Different sizes for every emergency. That's what he told me.'

When she replaced the receiver, her father called her. 'There's a native waiting for you. Says he's from the medical school. Says he's come to collect some notes.'

'Oh God! Dennis! I'd forgotten about him! I've got his notes. Here they are. Where is he? When did he come?'

'About twenty minutes ago.'

'Oh! As long as that. Where is he?'

'I sent him round the back. He's in the yard.'

'The yard? Why did you do that? He's a medical student.'

'I don't care what he is. I don't want any natives at the front door.'

Maryssa rushed to the kitchen. 'Where is he?' she asked.

The girl motioned with her head and answered, 'Outside,' and stirred the rice.

He was standing in the dark yard rubbing his hands together, his breath steaming, a cold wind whipping at his jacket.

'Dennis! I'm so sorry! I didn't know you were here. Please come in. I've done your notes.'

'Don' worry, mizz.' He put his hands together, palms touching, in a gesture of gratitude. He smiled, but his face was gaunt and grey. From his jacket pocket he unrolled a ten-shilling note. 'For you, mizz. For all your work. It helps me ver' much. I don' know how to say thanks to you for what you help me.'

'Oh. No, I don't want your money. Please…I'm pleased I could help. But you look so cold. Have a cup of tea before you go. And something to eat. You must be hungry. I'll make you a sandwich.'

'No thanks. For sure, I mus' go. I still mus' get back to my home. I got a lot to study tonight.'

'Are you sure?' She studied his face. He looked worn out. 'Well. OK. You've got the notes.'

'Yes. Bye, mizz. Thanks again.' He held up his hand and walked down the lane, a thin figure against the black night.

She waited until he was gone into the cold wind, into the long road, into the lonely journey that he took – each day, twice a day.

She remembered how long he had been made to wait in the bone-chilling darkness. She was angry with herself for not having been there to answer the door. She thought of the indignities her father had forced on this man, of the dismissive and disrespectful way he'd behaved towards him.

Filled with a sense of overwhelming frustration, she stood before him and shouted, 'Why did you do that? Why on earth did you do that? Sending him to the back! Making him stand in the freezing cold! Do you know how cold it is outside? Tell me! Why did you do that? Why?' Her face was taut, her hands clenched. She, who never challenged her father, who always tried to keep him quiet and calm, was now consumed with helplessness. Tears fell from her eyes, ran down her cheeks.

He, surprisingly, remained calm. He glanced at her, then fixed his gaze on the newspaper. 'I told you.' His voice was ominously quiet. 'I don't want any natives at the front door. Do you understand me. No *schwarzes* are allowed through the front door.'

Then he looked up at her and said loudly and with emphasis, 'I don't give a damn who they are.'

*E*llis. Come for supper.

 Ellis. It's getting ice cold. Come an' eat.

 Ellis. Where are you? The food's getting cold. Come to the table. Oh, where is he? His food is ice-cold.

What's this?

 Fricadels.

 Fricadels? Again?

 What do you mean again? We had them a week ago.

 A week ago? We had them last night.

 No. Last night we had curry.

 Don't tell me we had curry! We had fricadels! This food is ice-cold.

 Well, it's been standing for ages. I called you and called you…

 I can't eat this. This is ice-cold. I can't eat ice-cold food. Bella! Come here! Warm this up. I can't eat this. It's ice-cold.

Where are you going?

 To the room. Call me when it's hot.

The food stays in Maryssa's mouth. She chews and chews but she can't swallow. It feels like a big ball in her mouth – a ball that will choke her if she attempts to swallow it.

Ellis. Ellis. Here's your food. Come now. It's hot. Come an' eat. For God's sake…

 It's burnt. Look how black it is.

 It's not burnt. It tastes very nice…

 It's black as coal. It's burnt. She burnt it. She's useless. That shikse's useless. She's not a cook's backside. I can't eat this. It's hard as a bladdy rock.

That's because she had to warm it. You can't keep putting food backwards and forwards in the oven.

I can't eat this. Every night fricadels! This is burnt. Get rid of this shikse. She's useless.

Ssh, Ellis. She can hear you…

I don't bladdy well care. There's nothing to eat in this place. This is shit. You give me this shit to eat. Throw it out. Throw this shit out!

He turns the plate upside down. Gravy oozes from under it. Oozes and spreads like running shit.

Oh, Ellis…

Shuddup. She's useless and you're useless. You're a useless woman! You're nothing but a bladdy useless woman!

He lurches from the table.

From behind the bedroom curtain, gold bubbles wink in the whisky goblet.

Did you ever hear from Justin after that evening? You know, after your matric dance?

No.

And Gerald? He seemed very keen on you…

I think he was… But no. I haven't heard from him lately.

And David? And Sam? What about Sam?

No! I haven't heard from any of them! Not one of them. Why are you asking me all these questions? You're upsetting me!

Hi, Maryssa

I'm in my car at the Pavilion watching the waves. It calms my mind after a really hectic day at the hospital.

As I sit here, you come strongly to mind.

I miss you.

I'm thinking of your holiday in Cape Town last December.

I'm thinking of the day we spent at the docks watching the boats come in and leave. I can feel my arms around you and the brush of your hair against my face.

I remember the party we went to where the guys dived for crayfish from their balcony and threw the fish into boiling water. I remember your hand in mine and how contented I felt having you near me.

And the afternoon we lay on the carpet at Stephen's place, all of us, listening to classical music. Did you know I was watching you? You wouldn't know. Your eyes were closed…

And the day we spent swimming at Boulders… And New Year's Eve at the Catacombs…

And that night, that unforgettable night we spent alone in Cyril's flat…

I miss you.

I need to see you again.

I really need to be with you again.

Soon.

As soon as possible.

Dan

A man struggles in the gutter trying to steady himself. He lurches and sways, oblivious to the jibes of two native women who stare at him.

'Yoh!' they cluck. 'So drunk!'

The people in the queue at the tram stop turn their faces and move away from him.

In a dreadful and despairing moment, Maryssa sees her father weaving precariously through the late afternoon home going crowd in the middle of Eloff Street. Her heart begins to hammer loudly. She becomes deaf to the sound of passing cars, the clatter of trams, the voices around her. Her face burns and her body seems cased in cement. She moves out of the queue before he sees her and runs without direction through the crowds, sobbing silently, in blind panic, block after block.

Her mother is waiting at the tram stop when she finally arrives home. It's dark and Maryssa is shivering.

'Where've you been? Why are you so late? I was very worried. You should have been home an hour ago! What happened?'

Maryssa, in that instant, chooses not to tell her, but asks instead, 'Is Dad home?'

'Yes,' her mother sighs. 'He's home. But he's been drinking. He's in a terrible mood.'

That incident stayed with her. The sight of her father weaving across the busy road in a drunken state, the fear of him falling, perhaps being run over, the angry hoots from cars, the embarrassment and the panic that surged through her as she tried to run, pushing against the surge of the five o'clock crowd, the compulsion to move away from him as far as possible, as quickly as she could – all those feelings remained with her. 'He could have been killed!' she'd cried.

There was a continual anxious gnawing in the pit of her stomach, a restlessness, and now at night she only managed to sleep for a few hours before waking, frightened, her hair damp, her body wet.

Betty was concerned. She saw the feverishness in Maryssa's eyes, their dark circles, the wide cheekbones in her pale face sharply defined. She tried to talk to her, but Maryssa was unable to say what was wrong.

Ellis, too, worried. He'd never seen his daughter like this. He did not see himself as the cause, but, nevertheless, made a great effort to hold himself in check – to be sober. He came to the table each evening attempting light conversation and silly jokes that seemed clumsy and awkward. Maryssa did not register what he was saying. She was finding difficulty in eating. She took small mouthfuls, chewed longer than necessary and then struggled to swallow. She tensely waited for the next outbreak of temper, the shouting, the insults, and the sad and silent tears in her mother's eyes. This attempt at peace did not assuage her. When she could sit no longer, she excused herself and went to her room, closed the door and huddled under her eiderdown, Daniel's letter clutched to her chest.

They made an appointment for her to see a doctor, but she refused to go. 'There are plenty of doctors at work,' she responded angrily. 'I see them every day. They haven't said anything. They haven't noticed anything wrong with me.'

But they did notice, and they commented, and, on a bright afternoon with the sun was streaming across his desk, Professor Stern asked to see her. His face was kind, his voice gentle, but his eyes were concerned. Maryssa was pale and wan. She'd lost weight.

'You should see a doctor, have some tests done.'

She shook her head.

'Maryssa? Is there anything bothering you?' He watched her carefully. 'Anything you want to talk about? Anything you want to tell me?'

Again she shook her head.

They were silent for a few moments. Maryssa looked at her hands, twisting her fingers together.

'Well, then…' The professor paused. 'Perhaps you need some time off. A break.'

Maryssa sat quietly. She listened.

'Perhaps you should go away for a while.'

She thought about what he'd said.

Go away…

She *could* go away.

She could go to Cape Town.

She could go to Daniel…

'Perhaps I should,' she said hesitantly.

'Of course you should! What a good idea!' The professor's face broke into a warm smile. 'Tell you what I'm going to do. I'm going to give you some time off – we'll call it sick leave. You'll be fully paid. Have a proper break. Get your strength back.'

Ted loaded her suitcase into the boot of his car and drove her to the train station. It was a crisp spring day under a washed blue sky. The trees in the broken pavements were wearing new green.

'So… You'll be away for three months?'

'Ja. I'll have a month off and then I'm going to work for a private pathologist for two months. His secretary's going overseas. Prof Stern organised all this for me. He's been fantastic.'

Maryssa thought of her boss, that funny-looking little man with his oversized forehead and nose that was too big for his face. She remembered his kind smile, his clever eyes, and the kindness he had shown her. She wanted to cry.

'I expect you'll be teaming up with Daniel?' Ted held the wheel with one hand, and a cigarette in the other.

'Ja. Hopefully.'

'You like him?'

'I do. Very much. But I'm not sure how he feels about me. He doesn't give much away.'

'Daniel? Always been a bit of a closed book. I've been friends with him since we were kids. He usually stays with me when he comes to Joey's…and I've stayed at his place a couple of times in Cape Town…'

'Oh, have you? I met his mom when I was last there. She seems very nice.'

'She is. A very nice woman. I believe she had a helluva time with his dad. From all accounts, he was a bad egg. They divorced years ago.'

'Does Dan see him?'

'His dad died. But even when he was alive, I don't think he saw much of him. He didn't like him. He told me he only has bad memories of him. He was quite traumatised as a kid by all the fighting. I think that's why he doesn't give much away. Then, after the divorce, he took on a lot of responsibility, helping his mom, looking after his sisters. He was always working in the school holidays to try and make a few bucks.'

Ted paused and looked at Maryssa. 'Your set-ups are quite similar, aren't they?'

'I suppose they are, in a way… Except for my parents. They have their issues, but they actually really do love each other.'

Then she said, 'Daniel seems very bright…'

'He's brilliant. Went right through medical school on scholarships. He was top of his class a lot of the time. He's a focused guy, single-minded, very ambitious. He's a really good guy. He'll go far. But he can be moody. He's got a helluva short fuse. Blows up a lot. Slightest thing sets him off.' Ted turned to her. 'Think you can handle that, Shmoe?'

Maryssa stared ahead. 'I don't know,' she answered. 'I hardly know him.' She paused then said, 'And I'm not thinking too far ahead.'

They walked along the crowded platform until they found her compartment. It was already occupied by five women with their suitcases and carrier bags.

Ted pushed her suitcase onto a rack above the seat. 'Well,' he smiled, 'looks like you won't be short of company.'

His elbows leaned against the outside of the window. There was a loud whistle. The train shuddered and all the doors were locked.

Ted took her hand. 'Time to go, little Shmoe. Look after yourself.'

'And you, Ted.' Her eyes filled with concern. 'You need to look after yourself. Please. You need to be careful.'

'Careful?' Ted said with the ghost of a smile. 'I know I'm carefree. And most of the time I'm careless. But careful? Don't know what the word means.'

She watched him walk away, his thin figure soon lost in the crowd. He went without looking back, but then, above the crowd she saw his hand wave, and he was gone.

Maryssa left the crowded compartment to stand in the passageway. The smell of cooked chicken and oranges followed her. She closed her eyes and heard the clicking of the wheels on the rails, felt the side to side movement of the train, the reverberations of the carriages as they sped along the tracks.

She watched the flat colourless countryside pass by – the scrubby trees, a few cows, a dog. At a barren station, an old man boarded with a battered suitcase. Behind him, a few sad houses slumped in dry gardens, lifeless except for washing blowing on lines. A lonely road carved into the veld and an abandoned truck stood desolate.

At each station, children ran to the train with outstretched arms and upturned pink palms, their brown legs bony and dusted with dirt.

But their smiles were white and their black eyes shone. With bobbing heads and clasped hands, they waited for half-eaten sandwiches and bruised fruit from the passengers. 'Thenks, missus! Thenks, maastah!' they sang as they skipped away laughing. Behind them sat their brooding mothers, and scrawny dogs skulked in the background.

It was in the darkness of the night, in the closed space of her bunk, that Maryssa put on a small night light and reread Daniel's letter.

'Yes,' she answered his words silently. 'Of course I remember. I remember it all…

'I remember the afternoon at the harbour. The wall was wide and warm. There was a huge liner on the quay. Foreign accents. A lot of loading and offloading. Your arms were around me, my hair blew in your face. "Leave it," you said. "I like it."

'I remember the night at the Catacombs, with that big fat native man who sang like Satchmo, who seemed to be singing just for us. We held onto each other when the music stopped. We didn't want to let go.

'I remember the party at Clifton and the crayfish brought up from the sea and over the balcony. They screamed when they were thrown into boiling water, and I clutched your hand. "They die immediately," you said. "They don't suffer much." But neither of us ate them. Not because of the way they were cooked. We discovered that neither of us ate any form of shellfish, or pork.

'And the night at your friend's flat – that small one-roomed flat that overlooked the bright lights of Main Road with the rush and tooting of cars, and the voices and laughter of people passing by. There was no curtain on the window and we saw each other as we were. We used the time slowly, kissing, exploring each other, revelling in the intense emotions and desires that engulfed us, not wanting the night to end…

'I remember the day I left. I watched the crowds on the platform hoping to see you. Even when the train pulled out, when the crowds became waving hands, I watched the blur of faces hoping to see yours. You never came…

'Then the telegram – "Daniel Simons MB CHB love Dan".

'And my response, "Congratulations Dr Simons".

'You said you'd write. That was last December…

'When your letter finally came, I was surprised to receive it. I'd waited so long…'

In her mind, she could see his dark eyes, his smile. She saw him standing, no, leaning against a doorpost, always leaning, with a faintly sardonic expression on his face that would then soften. His eyes would become warm and tender, and he would look deeply into hers and talk to her with his eyes. No words. Just that deep warm look.

The train was taking her to him, to that city by the sea, that city enfolded in the curved flanks of a giant flat topped mountain, that place where two oceans meet, one warm, one cold, and merge and flow together, and become one. At the southern tip of Africa, at the point of the Cape Peninsula.

Cape Town.

In the arms of Table Mountain.

She woke early, slipped into the little bathroom at the end of the carriage and held on to the door with one hand to balance against the rolling movement of the train, washing herself with water that sloshed from side to side in the basin.

From the passageway, she watched the sun, a huge orange ball, rising in an unblemished sky. The veld that rolled out to meet the horizon was flat except for low flat-topped *koppie*s. The sandy soil, punctuated with clumps of grey brush, seemed to glow in the bright sunlight. There was an occasional burst of colour from a hardy flowering Karoo bush, an occasional bird flying high. A few sheep grazed near a dilapidated wind pump. The air was dry and carried shrouds of dust.

Maryssa remembered her mother and sisters pressed against the lounge window, the sad smile that her mother summonsed, the confusion on the faces of her sisters. Why was she going away? their expressions asked. What was wrong? What had happened? What was any different to what had always been?

Their sadness became her sadness. She wondered if her mother had played her only record, *The Bluebird of Happiness*, after she left. This was what her mother did when she felt overwhelmed. The words of the song seemed to help her, to bring her comfort.

But Maryssa knew that she had to go away, to remove herself from that sadness. She was already feeling less stressed. She'd slept well and woke refreshed. For the first time in a long while, she was hungry. Having given away her sandwiches to the picanninnies, those hungry children with their huge black eyes and upturned pink palms, she remembered that she had only eaten an apple since she'd been on the train.

When the breakfast sessions were over, she left her crowded compartment and sat at a table in the dining carriage. She ordered an orange juice, toast and tea. The juice was delicious, freshly squeezed with bits of orange in it, and the toast was warm and crisp. She ate and drank, savouring each mouthful, then gazed out of the window sipping tea. She felt happy and excited and peaceful, all at once.

Towards noon, the train approached the town of Worcester. The arid and barren Karoo was left behind. They were now approaching the famous wine-growing region of the Cape. Ahead, the mountain ranges of the Swartberg and Langeberg loomed majestically, and in the folds of their lower slopes nestled vineyards and orchards, like a vast patchwork quilt. A farmhouse, startlingly white, with matching curved gables and low white walls stood clearly against a background of purple-grey mountain and workers could be seen moving among the vines.

They were only an hour or two away from Cape Town. Maryssa knew that she would soon begin to smell the sea, that salty briny smell that was carried by sea winds.

The Geneva Hotel called itself a family hotel. In reality, it was more like a youth hostel, filled with young people from other cities who chose to study or work in Cape Town. Situated in the heart of Sea Point, it was close to the shops, and the bus stop was half a corner away. The main building was plain and squat, housing a large lounge and a very large dining room that was furnished with long communal dining tables. You sat wherever there was space and three roving waiters served you when you raised your hand. Of course, when the dining room was full, you'd wait a long time for your next course.

The food was plain but satisfactory. What was disappointing were the desserts. In the summer, guavas were bought in large crates, and stewed guavas were served at breakfast, lunch and dinner every evening until the guava season was over.

But the atmosphere was always jolly, the young people joking about the service and the guavas, exchanging news, and always on the lookout for new arrivals – a pretty girl, or a good-looking boy.

Attached to the hotel were two annexes, old houses that had been converted into bedrooms and communal bathrooms. They were identical buildings, each with single and double rooms and long dark passages that went from the front entrance in straight lines to the ends of the houses. The rooms facing east received a lick of sunlight in the early mornings, those facing west a blush of late afternoon sun, but as the residents were out for most of the time, the gloom of their rooms went largely unnoticed.

At the end of the passage in the second annexe, a short passage turned right passed a bathroom to the smallest room. It was thought to have originally been a pantry. This room was the only one to face north, and, with its wide window and no outside obstructions such as walls or trees, the sun was free to enter and painted the walls with sunlight from early morning until the last pale rays of day faded away.

This room was rented to Maryssa. A single bed covered with a white and blue striped counterpane, a small side table next to the bed, a set of drawers, a narrow wardrobe and a straight-backed chair fitted compactly into the space. In one corner was a washbasin and a towel rack, and above that a mirror nailed to the wall.

Tucked away at the back of the building, the little room was a light and warm space, a comforting space, unadorned and plain, from which emanated peace during the day and a dark cloak of peace through the long hours of the night.

For the first few days, Maryssa absorbed the stillness of this space. She came back from her walks, rested in the afternoons, and spent the quiet evenings watching the sky change colour and the stars come out. It was the time of the full moon and the moon hung huge and luminous, casting its white light through the window and across her.

In the hours that drifted by like clouds, Maryssa slowly regained a sense of well-being. She bathed each evening after supper, went to bed early, enjoyed deep and restful sleep, and woke at dawn feeling cool and refreshed. The dark circles under her eyes faded and her eyes regained their sparkle. Gentle colour, like the skin of a pale peach, suffused her cheeks and her face began to lose its sharp angles, becoming soft and pretty again.

As she became more at home in the room, she dressed it with small bunches of flowers and shells she found on the beach. Her perfume bottles and little pots of creams and lotions were grouped and displayed on the chest of drawers, next to a bowl of glowing sweet-smelling late season apples. A white cardigan hung on the back of the chair. Her dressing-gown was draped over the end of the bed. A library book lay open on the small table. Her slippers were under it. The perfume of Maryssa, the scent of flowers and the scent of apples mingled.

The essence of Maryssa suffused the room. Without being conscious of it, she'd made it hers.

She surprised herself by waiting a week before she contacted Daniel.

On the train, she'd planned to phone him as soon as she arrived, and had gone to the public phone booth to do so. She dialled his number, let it ring twice and then replaced the receiver. Overcome by a sense of unease, she'd wondered how he would feel about her. Would he still like her? Would he want to be with her?

Their first meeting felt strange. She sat on the bed, he on the chair. They tried to make conversation but their words were stilted and the time they spent together uncomfortable. He stayed for a short while then said that he had to go. He had a lot of work to get through before the next day – records and reports to update. She said she understood. They hugged awkwardly and he left without saying that he would be in touch.

She waited, hoping desperately each day that he would phone. His letter had been so encouraging. It was because of the letter that she'd decided to come to Cape Town. He'd said that he wanted to see her, that he wanted to be with her. But now he seemed to have lost interest in their relationship.

One evening after not having heard him since his brief visit, she had an overwhelming urge to hear his voice. She hesitated, then plucked up courage to dial his number.

When he heard her on the line, he was silent. Then he shouted, 'Maryssa. Don't do this! Don't phone me!' and banged down the receiver.

She was shocked and frightened by his reaction, and confused that he should be so angry with her.

But the next evening he came to see her. He was warm and gentle. He held her and kissed her. She was filled with joy and excitement. He was again the person that she remembered.

Neither of them referred to the phone call. He was probably stressed and exhausted, she told herself, trying to understand what had caused him to act in that way. She excused him and forgave him, but, recalling how shocked she was at his reaction, she resolved never to dial his number again.

Daniel made it quite clear that he would not be tied down. He was casual and erratic about their relationship. He would see her when it suited him, sometimes quite frequently; and then, for no reason, not for days on end.

She reminded herself that he was busy, that he did not owe her anything, and that he had not given her any indication of how he felt about her. But her feelings for him were intense. She wanted to be with him. It was difficult for her to accept dates from some of the other young men who showed an interest in her.

When Daniel was not with her, she preferred to be alone.

She filled her days by accepting an offer to type a thesis for a PhD student who lived in the building opposite the hotel. Each morning she let herself his flat, and opened the windows wide to let out the smell of stale bed linen, an odour from unwashed clothes and the stink from an old pair of trackies. Occasionally he did what he laughingly called a big clean-up but, he said, by his own admission he was not big on domesticity.

Each morning, she scrubbed one of the stained mugs from the sink, made tea and sat at the desk by the window from where she could see London Road – the passing cars, the people and the entrance to the hotel.

Each evening, the student would correct his work, asking her to type the same pages over again. But she was paid for each page, and, as the errors and changes were his, she did not mind repeating what she'd done the day before.

On most afternoons, Maryssa walked along the promenade. She would sometimes go towards Cape Town, passing the tiny harbour in Green Point from where motorboats launched.

One bright crisp day, a man, a stranger, asked her whether she would like to go out on his boat. Without thinking, she agreed. He helped her to board, the motor roared and the boat sprang to life, riding the waves like a bucking bronco. Maryssa clung to the sides, doing all she could to stop herself from falling out.

They arrived at Clifton and from the sparkling blue of the ocean she saw the curve of the white beach and the dark cliff beyond.

'That is beautiful,' she said.

They then turned round and sped back, bouncing along wildly on the waves until they reached the little harbour. She clambered out of the boat, thanked the man for the ride and walked off, very pleased to be back on firm ground.

When she told a friend at the hotel where she'd been, the girl retorted with some concern, 'What! Are you mad! Going with a perfect stranger onto a boat! You could have been raped! He could have raped you and thrown you overboard! You could have been murdered…'

Maryssa thought about what she'd said. 'She's right,' she told herself. 'I shouldn't have done that.'

‘It's really hot tonight,’ said Daniel. ‘Let's go for a swim.’
As they drove towards Sunrise Beach, the lights of houses were left behind, the road became lonely, and beige sand dunes piled one upon the other, lit only by the beam of a flat moon.

At the beach, the empty parking lot flattened before them, and the café and change rooms were boarded and locked with bolts and chains. The beach, deserted, wide in low tide, was silky beneath their feet. Waves, delicately plumed and highlighted by moonbeams, licked the shore.

‘I know this beach,’ Maryssa said. ‘I remember coming here as a child – I was about four or five – with my mom. We came on holiday. The war was nearly over, but my dad couldn't come. He was still in the Home Guard.’

She shivered in the silence of the huge space of black sea and sky. ‘Are you really going in there? It looks so ominous.’

Daniel grinned and stripped, leaving his clothes in a pile beside her. He ran into the water, into a stream of moonlight. Feeling cold and nervous, she slipped her arms into his shirt sleeves and pulled the shirt tightly around her as she watched him diving into the waves. Then he disappeared from the light into impregnable darkness.

Anxious, she walked towards the water, looking for him. Afraid, she said aloud, ‘Where is he? For God's sake! Where the hell is he?’

After a few minutes, he appeared, wet and pale, and ran towards her.

‘Oh! Thank God,’ she gasped. ‘You gave me such a fright! I couldn't see you…’

’It was fantastic. You should have come in. You'd have loved it! Come! Let's run. I need to warm up!’

He grabbed her hand and together they ran along the vast stretch of lonely beach. Laughing, they dropped onto the sand. His mouth found hers and she held his wet body close to her.

'Hi, sweetheart,' he whispered.

'Dan, let's go back. Please. It's really ghostly here…'

They ran back to the pile of clothes, to their shoes that stood out starkly on the white sand.

He took his shirt from her and felt the pocket. 'Hey,' he asked, 'where's my watch. Have you got my watch? It was in my pocket.'

'Your watch? No, I don't have it.'

'It was in my pocket. It must have fallen out. You've lost my watch!'

'You never told me it was in your pocket.'

'God! You've lost it. That watch cost me a year's salary! Didn't you feel it in my pocket? It's a big heavy watch! How could you not know it was there?' He scrabbled in the sand. 'You're really stupid, you know! What a stupid woman!'

Maryssa, stunned, her heart beating loudly, her hand to her throat, followed him as he retraced their footsteps in the sand. She cringed at the sharp staccato tones in his voice, at the angry tensing of his shoulders.

In the white light of the moon, they moved carefully, focusing on the still sand, not wanting to disturb it, not wanting a shower of sand to cover their prints.

It was where they had lain that they found it, round and heavy, encased in platinum, like a small moon gazing up at the sky.

'Jesus!' he exclaimed. 'Wow! Lucky…really lucky we found it! I would have been devastated.'

'You should have given to me. I would have put it on my wrist…' Her voice was small and broken.

'I've found it. That's the important thing. I've got it back!' He grinned and his anger was gone.

They drove back through the quiet streets and onto De Waal Drive, where the street lights stretched below them like a sapphire necklace, but she did not see them. She glanced at his wrist, at the watch, at the leather strap, and looked away, her hands clenched in her lap.

Did Daniel realise how his words had shocked her? Did he see her taut face? Did he feel her shrink away from him? Had he automatically used those words that he'd heard so often in his past, those damning heartless words so often spoken by his father in a loud aggressive voice? In his own sudden anger and frustration, did those words come without thought. 'You're stupid, you know! You're really stupid!' Were they imprinted from childhood? Were they a part of him despite him running away from them, despite him hiding from them?

'You're so stupid, you silly bitch. God knows how I ended up with you? What a stupid silly bitch. Your mother's a silly bitch. Did you know that? A stupid silly bitch.'

Were those words imprinted in the mind of a small boy who ran from the room and buried his head under the pillow? A small boy who clenched his jaw and clamped his lips into a thin line, yet did not manage to hold back the tears that flowed, and who finally fell asleep, his pale cheeks against a patch of salty wetness.

Would Rebecca announce, 'Ma, Daniel's wet his bed again!'

Would he scream, 'I did not!'

'Oh yes, you did. I went to feel. You peed in the bed again.'

And from his mother crossly, 'Stop it, Rebecca. It doesn't matter. It was an accident.'

Did the small boy with clamped jaw and tight lips hide his wet pyjamas and stamp to the bathroom to wash away the smell?

Had the words that had been hurled so often at his mother become imprinted in his subconscious mind? Had they become a part of who he was?

Because this was not the first time Maryssa had seen Daniel's jaw tighten and his lips set in a straight thin line. It was not the first time that he'd reacted with sharp staccato words that wounded her deeply. It was not the first time that his eyes drained of all sparkle and became dark lifeless stones.

It was not the first time that he'd lost his temper with her, leaving her feeling empty, insecure and afraid.

The telegram arrived a few weeks later. It read, 'Darling. Very sad news. Ted found dead in his car. So sorry. Love Ma.'

Leaning against the sea wall, she reads the note again. The waves blur and the ground wavers. She's unaware of people passing, of passing traffic. She does not see the cold sea or the harsh grey sky. She stares woodenly ahead. 'Ted is dead, Ted is dead,' echoes through her mind. 'Ted, my friend, is dead. Ted? Ted dead? Ted is dead.'

Ted, whose hair fell over his forehead, whose fingers were stained with nicotine, is dead…

Ted, who was filled with compassion, who felt more deeply than anyone she'd ever known, who stood before a crowded auditorium and cried, 'We have to fight for the rights of all humans,' is dead.

The air is cold and still. Sea and sky blend together to form a grey screen. She recalls the words he wrote on her cigarette box:

> Black and white are each too strong –
> They have never got along…

And when he said with sadness in his voice, and sadness in the long lines of his face, and sadness in the slump of his shoulders, 'Sometimes you just have to walk away…'

She began to realise that a part of Ted had faded a while ago, on that dark night, in the light of a silver moon, as they lay together beside a silver river.

Daniel was devastated. 'I can't believe it! Ted! One of my best buddies… An amazing guy! An amazing intellect. So empathic. So compassionate. Looking out for everyone but himself…'

Maryssa told Daniel that she'd noticed that at times Ted seemed a bit down, a bit depressed. There was talk that he'd committed suicide, but that she thought that he would not take his own life.

'Neither do I,' Daniel responded. 'He was a strong guy in every way. Very dedicated. But he was playing with fire. He was blacklisted. He was definitely being watched... We'll never know, of course, because the police are not going to go out of their way to find out what really happened to him. He refused to heed the warning signs. He was a thorn in their side. Who knows? Perhaps they wanted to get rid of him… They might have done the job themselves…'

They drove along De Waal Drive towards the hospital. The double carriage way was quiet after the surge of evening traffic. The sky bulged with black clouds and street lamps glittered, highlighting the roads all the way to the northern suburbs. The mountain was dark and tall pines made darker shadows against its flanks. The air was still and a mist began to cloud the windscreen.

'The bucks have come down. They're at the fence,' she said.

The animals huddled in close groups, their antlers white boned. Lightning bleached the clouds and an ominous rumble of thunder rolled in loudly from the distance.

'Looks like we're in for a huge storm.'

'I hope it doesn't start before we get there. I don't like driving when there's lightning. I'm scared it'll strike me.'

'Not likely. It's sheet lightning, not forked..'

'It still terrifies me. The storms in Jo'burg were really scary. You can see the lightning strike the road. There would be reports of people who were killed. Some poor guy or woman who took shelter under a tree in the veld...'

'That's the worst place to stand.'

Another violet crash of blinding white light flashed across the sky. The clouds burst and rain poured down in torrents. The car swung into the parking area.

'We'll have to run for it.' He turned to her. 'Are you ready?'

The hospital loomed, massive, inconsistent in its varied shapes of old and new buildings. The lights were dimmed in the wards and the entrance to the doctors' residence. They ran hand in hand through the doors, rain beading their hair, with wet faces and drenched shoulders.

'Wow! What a downpour! I'm soaked! We need to dry off. Come to my room and we'll change into something dry. Then I'll grab my white coat and I'll show you around my ward.'

It was the first time she'd been into his doctor's room. The small space was neat, the desk piled with books. A lamp gave a warm golden light.

'Here, grab this towel. And put this shirt on…'

She rubbed her hair and folded it turban style, into the towel, unbuttoned her blouse, slipped it off and hung it on the back of a chair, pulled on his shirt and sat laughing, cross-legged, on his bed.

Rubbing his hair with a handkerchief, he leaned against his desk watching her undo the turban, the sleeves of his shirt dropping back from her wrists revealing her bare arms, Her hair fell in thick wet strands and her face was suffused with warm colour. She met his long intense gaze and smiled.

'You look sexy, you know.' His voice was husky, his eyes dark. 'Very sexy…'

She'd caught his attention when she was seventeen in the dim light of that room filled with the beat of 'Blue Suede Shoes' and the crowd who moved to it. He'd watched the light play on her hair – red and gold lights, he saw the curve of her cheek, the lift of her chin, the swaying of her, her square shoulders – and he was captured.

He liked to listen to her warm expressive voice with its gentle cadences, her short unembroidered sentences. Maryssa preferred to listen. She listened with her eyes, tawny eyes that absorbed and reflected what she had heard. She listened with her mouth, with lips that parted and smiled and revealed white even teeth. She listened with her hands that clasped and unclasped, or were held together, palm to palm, as if in prayer. He wanted to kiss the hollow of her throat, to cover her prayerful hands with his own, to lean into the warmth of her.

But he also wanted to break away. In his clinical way, he'd always been in charge. This girl with thick auburn hair made him uneasy. He'd achieved his goals because of his clear focus and unencumbered emotions. He could allow himself to like a girl, and then, without effort, move away from her. Liking a girl was slotted into his other activities, like listening to his music, and then put aside, much in the same way as he replaced his violin after he'd played it. Enjoying a girl's company was for the time allotted. It did not encroach.

But Maryssa was different. She infiltrated his thoughts at unannounced times – as he pushed his chair away from his desk, or strode through the hospital corridors, or drove along De Vaal Drive. He found himself remembering her arms as she leaned on a table holding her cup in both hands, the curve of her crossed thighs, the curve of her lips. His thoughts were intense and invasive, and he became frustrated trying to dismiss them. He was angry with himself, with his loss of control. His anger was reflected in the way he sometimes treated her, shouting at her, becoming uncommunicative, removing himself. She, in turn, was confused and perplexed. Then he would see the suffering in her eyes and he, too, would suffer, and regret his behaviour. His resentment would disappear, and he'd feel overcome with warmth for her. His face would soften and his eyes become deep dark pools smiling at her, and all was said with no words spoken.

Maryssa forgave him. She forgave his loss of temper, his sharp clipped tone of voice, his seeming lack of concern. She loved him. She wanted to be with him. She wanted him to want her.

As he wanted her – in his room, in the darkness of her small room- two young people, naked and pale, blended together as one.

Although they did not indulge fully, their lovemaking was complete. The excitement they evoked from each other was electric, and it was easy for them to reach the ultimate heights of ecstasy, and to be left exhausted but replete in each others' arms, gently touched by moonlight.

But it was the intensity of their feelings that disturbed Daniel. He could not allow his true feelings to take over. He could not allow himself to become distracted. 'Absolutely not!' he told himself. I've got a lot to do. I've got to specialise. I can't get involved here. I can't let this happen. I have to move away from it. Now.'

In the lounge of the hotel, the young men stretched their legs and leaned their heads against the backs of couches and armchairs.

David Finkelstein's eyes were half-closed as he hitched his leg over the arm of his chair. 'So…tell me, Danny…what's up with this girlfriend of yours?'

'Who?' Daniel kept his voice disinterested.

'You know. Your girlfriend. Maryssa.'

'My girlfriend? She's not my girlfriend. Who says she's my girlfriend?'

'I thought she was. We all,' and he nodded to the others 'thought she was.'

'Shows you how wrong you can be. I mean, I see her from time to time… But girlfriend? No. She's not my girlfriend.'

'Does that mean that she goes out with other guys beside you?' David asked casually but his mind was now alert.

'Sure she does.' Then he said, 'Don't ask me. How would I know?' Daniel shifted in his chair and ran his fingers through his hair. The conflict of wanting her and not wanting the responsibility of having her was rising again within him.

He felt their eyes on him. They waited for him to continue. There was a silence.

He looked away. 'I mean, if you want to take her out, that's fine with me.'

'You mean you wouldn't mind?' David's eyes were fixed on him.

'Me? Mind? Of course not. Not at all. Go ahead. If you want to. Ask her out.' He shrugged and struggled to meet his friend's gaze.

'But Dan. She seems set on you. You can see the way she looks at you.'

Daniel shifted again. He wanted to move away from their seemingly casual scrutiny, from the talk about him and Maryssa, from his own uneasiness. 'Maybe she looks at all the guys like that. Maybe that's her way.'

'You mean that hot come-on look isn't just for you?' laughed Brian Cohen.

'Why should it only be for me? She probably uses it on all the guys.' He tried to grin. 'She's quite a little number…'

The boys drew their legs inwards towards them.

David pushed himself up and leaned forward. 'Sooo…' He focused his gaze on Daniel. 'So, if I wanted to take her out, maybe try her out? You'd be OK with that?'

'I told you. Do as you please.' Daniel stood up and stretched. 'Gotta go, guys. My mother's made supper. You know how mothers are… And I'm starving. Well, see you around.' He winked and, grinning, said, 'Good luck, Finks. Let me know how you make out.'

As Daniel drove away, he saw the back of Maryssa in the foyer of the hotel. This is the way to go, he thought. Let the other guys have a piece of her. In that way, she would discredit herself in his eyes, become diminished, a snide and sneering talking point, and the irritating persistent feelings he had for her would dissipate. He didn't need this in his life. He had enough to do without thoughts of this girl nagging away at him. Yes. This was definitely the way to go. Hopefully she'll spread herself around, and maybe next time he sees Finks they'll be able to have a real old good laugh about it.

Without thinking, he drove towards the city. His usually dry hands were clammy and he opened the window, needing air. Then he said, 'Where am I? What am I doing? What the hell…' And then, 'Oh well, I'm on the way there.'

He continued along De Waal Drive towards the hospital. Staring ahead, he was unaware of the rush of traffic, the brightness of headlights. He moved his tongue around his dry lips. Do a ward round. That's what he would do. Look in on the Fourie kid in Ward 4. He glanced at his watch. Ten past six. He'd left the hospital only an hour before. This was his night off.

But that's where he wanted to be, where he needed to be — concentrating, focusing, anything that would make him forget the conversation he'd just had with the guys in the lounge of the hotel.

L eech handed Maryssa her room key.

'No messages for me?' She smiled at his smile.

'No message, Mizz Kiein.'

'Nothing?' She waited, hoping that Leech was mistaken, that perhaps Daniel had phoned, that perhaps she would see him that evening.

He shook his head, watching her face with kindness, his eyes crinkling in his black face. He did not say that Daniel had just left, had walked past seconds before.

'Well, thanks. If...' she said hurriedly, 'if Dr Simons phones, will you please tell him I've gone for a walk and I'll phone him as soon as I get back.'

The foyer was beginning to fill with people waiting for the dining room doors to open. A smell of fried fish wafted from the kitchen.

The evening was warm and the sky was painted in glorious shades of red and orange. In the distance, a flock of birds formed a pattern of tiny black dots. Maryssa walked by the sea wall and felt the faint sea spray on her face. There was the wide ocean, the sharp smell of seaweed and the taste of salt in the air. On her left the outline of the mountain was ruggedly carved against a darkening sky and a pale sliver of moon appeared over Lion's Head.

Outside the hotel entrance, David sat in his car. His head lay on the back of his seat, his hands leisurely holding the steering wheel, his knee propped up against it. He'd loosened his tie and undone the top button of his shirt. He was waiting.

'Aren't you coming, Dave? Your favourite tonight. I can smell it from here. Fried fish...' his friends from the flats asked.

'Not my favourite.' His answer was gruff. They were blocking his view of the road. He was watching out for Maryssa.

'Not anybody's favourite… But a man's got to eat. You know what they say – a hungry man is an angry man.'

'I hate that fish! I'd rather be angry.'

Then he saw her. He saw the glow of her hair in the reflection of the red sky, her square shoulders and the jutting movement of her hips as she walked up the hill, and, when she passed, he leaned towards the passenger window. 'Hi,' he smiled. 'Howz it?'

'Fine, thanks. And you?'

'I'm fine. Did you go for a walk?'

'Ja. It was lovely.'

'It's a really nice evening. Have you eaten?'

'No. I'm going in now.'

'Well, hang on for me. We'll go in together.'

Maryssa waited, unsure that this was what she wanted to do. 'To tell the truth, I'm not that hungry.'

'Well, at least sit with me while I eat. I need company,' he smiled.

'Oh. OK.'

He turned to her. 'Tell you what. I don't fancy that fish. Let's go for a hamburger up the road. Tony's does a really good one.'

'David, I'm really not hungry.'

'Come with me. Keep me company. I don't want to eat alone. Come on…'

'I don't think so. I'm expecting a call.'

'You can phone back. We won't be away long.'

She walked to reception. 'Any calls for me?'

'No mizz, nothing,' and, disappointed, she turned away. He hadn't phoned for almost a week.

'OK. I'll come…'

David noted the darkening of her eyes, the downturn of her mouth, the twisting of her fingers, and, determined to divert her, he walked beside her talking of mundane things. He kept the conversation going as he ate, smiled, and told her a funny story of a customer who came into the pharmacy, and more funny stories until she laughed aloud, and the cloud lifted from her face, and she ate the hot chips he'd put on a side plate for her.

The sun had set and there was a slight chill in the air as they walked back.

'That was nice,' she said. 'It was fun. Thanks.'

'No. Thank you. It was great having you with me. You're a really good listener. Did you know that?'

'Well, you're a really good talker,' she laughed.

Then she thought of Daniel. 'I know so little about him,' she mused. He would look at her intently, expressively, and talk to her with love in his eyes. He'd smile his thin smile and take her hand in his warm dry grasp. But he never spoke about himself, about his work, about his family. She also remembered his anger, his vociferous outbursts of temper, the tightening of his jaw.

David saw that she was confused and upset. He knew why. It was almost time for his to make his move, he told himself. Almost time…

It was on Saturday morning that she could no longer bear waiting for his call. Against her better judgement, she phoned from the hotel call box.

He shouted, 'How did you know I was here?'

'I didn't... I tried your number...' she said apologetically.

'Well, don't do that again.' His voice was cold. 'I told you not to phone me. I'm really busy. I have to go.'

Disconsolately, she turned from the telephone. Her eyes filled with tears.

David was standing there. 'Hey?' he asked with a kind expression on his face. 'What's up?'

'Nothing,' she answered. She tried to pass but he gently took her arm.

'Don't tell me that. I can see you're upset. Aren't you feeling well?'

'I'm OK.'

'Sure?'

'Yes. I'm really OK.'

He said, 'Hey, look. I'm really pleased I've bumped into you. I've got two comps for the Hofmeyr for *Bus Stop*. You know – the Tennessee Williams play. They say it's great. If you're not going out tonight, why don't you come with me?'

Numbly and without thinking she replied, 'Tonight? Um...that's sounds nice. Thanks. I will come.'

'OK. Tonight then.' David was delighted. This had fallen into his lap. 'Shows you,' he grinned to himself. 'Perfect timing. Right place, right time... Well, let's see how this pans out...'

In the dark of the theatre, she sat with her arms folded and moved away from him when his shoulder touched hers. But David was not discouraged. He told himself that she was shy. She needed a little warming up. He knew how to do that. He'd park at the beach front after the show and make his moves. It would be easy. Like taking sweets from a baby.

They drove back towards the hotel. 'It's a beautiful night. Just look at that moon!' he said as he turned the car into the deserted parking lot. 'Let's sit here for a while. Fantastic, isn't it!'

Maryssa stared ahead, remote and removed. Her thoughts were with Daniel. Her delicate perfume excited David. He watched her still profile, saw the fullness of her mouth and the thick fall of her hair. He slipped his arm along the back of her seat.

'David,' she said softly, 'I hope you don't mind. It's been a very nice evening but I'd really like to go back to the hotel.'

He leaned towards her and tried to kiss her.

'Please don't do that.' She turned her face away.

He slipped his arm around her shoulders and moved across the seat. He touched her breast.

'Don't do that. I said, don't do that.' Her voice was raised. She pushed his hand away. 'I want to go home. Take me back to the hotel.'

'Don't be silly, Maryssa.' His voice was gruff. 'You know you want it as much as I do…' His hand was on her thigh.

'Stop it,' she cried. 'Stop that. Get off me. Get away from me!'

He forced his lips on hers, tried to push his tongue into her mouth, turning his body onto hers.

Twisting her head from side to side, she shouted. 'Let me go! Let me out. Leave me alone. Let me out of this car…' She pushed the car door open and tried to get out.

They were no longer alone. Another car was parked further along. It put on its headlights and David noticed the darkened heads of two people looking in their direction.

Quickly he moved away from her. 'OK. OK,' he gulped. 'Don't panic. Calm down. What's with the hysteria? I'll take you back. For God's sake! What is it with you?' He turned on the ignition and, giving her a quick glance, drove back to the road.

Her face was pale. Her hands were shaking. He was unnerved by her. He now wanted to be rid of her. He wanted her out of his car as soon as possible.

At the hotel, she opened the car door without saying anything, rushed into the brightly lit foyer, took her key and a note from Leech, ran up the street and into the annexe, and down the long dark corridor. She panicked as she dropped her key outside her door, unlocked the door and locked it from the inside and tried it to make sure it was secure. She sank onto her bed, her head in her hands. Her heart was beating rapidly and the blood had drained from her face.

She saw her reflection in the mirror. She was pale and dishevelled. Her make up was smudged. She was shaking. Her eyes filled with tears. Trembling, she lit a cigarette.

The note lay at her feet. She stared at it, then picked it up. She read that Daniel had come to the hotel to see her, and that he had also phoned.

Much as he tried to fight them, Daniel's feelings for Maryssa engulfed him. Her image was constantly with him. He envisaged her tawny eyes that were soft and filled with love for him. He could feel the thickness of her hair, the small of her back. He could taste the softness of her lips.

He'd not spoken to her for a week, and he wondered if David, in that time, had made any headway. An unpleasant feeling rose in him and he decided that he would see David and tell him that the deal was off, that Maryssa was his girlfriend, that they were involved. He would tell him that she should not be asked out by David or, in fact, by any of the other guys.

'The sooner I sort this out the better,' he muttered to himself.

It was a busy afternoon in the wards. As time passed, his uneasiness grew and he was impatient to leave. He drove faster than usual to the hotel.

'Hi, Leech. Howz it? Miss Klein. Is she in?'

'No, doctor. No, she out. Gone. A few minutes ago.'

'Oh… Do you know where she went?'

'No, sir. I don'.'

'Who was she with?'

'That also I don' know…'

Daniel turned from the desk, then said, 'Is David Finkelstein in?'

'Don' know, doctor. I can try his room… Sorry, doctor. No reply… Any message?'

'No. Not for David. But please make sure to tell Miss Klein I called.'

'Yes sir, doctor. I will write the message for her.'

'Thanks. See you, Leech.'

'Good evenin', doctor sir.'

Leech had seen Maryssa leave with David. He noted everything that passed his desk but had long learned not to give anything away. He wrote the message for her and also took the phone call from Daniel later that evening wanting to know if Miss Klein was back. He saw the state Maryssa was in when she returned from her date with David, and David's avoidance of eye contact with him when he collected his key.

'She upset. Mr Finks also upset. Maybe they fight. But how she with him? She doctor's girl. Not Mr Finks's girl. She's a nice girl Mizz Klein. Look like they mess with her. Haai! These boys! They *skelms…*'

Maryssa woke when the sun was high and the room hot. Her head ached. She'd not fallen asleep until the first grey light had crept through the window. She pushed the covers from her, opened the window wide and drew the curtain against the sun's harsh rays. Stumbling to the basin, she splashed cold water onto her face and brushed her teeth with vigour. Her reflection was pale and drawn.

Last night's date with David flashed back vividly in her mind. She recalled with revulsion how he tried to force his tongue into her mouth, how he'd tried to touch her.

She wondered whether he would tell his friends. What he would tell them. What would he tell Daniel? She should never have accepted the date. David was Daniel's friend. What would David say about her? What would Daniel think of her?

She brushed her hair, pulled on slacks and a blouse and grabbed her sunglasses and key. She had to get out of the room. It seemed to be closing in on her.

She walked swiftly up the road, turned right into Main Street and walked towards the only person she wanted to see, to be with, to talk to – the person who, aside from her mother, would give her comfort.

Her aunt, Esther.

The sun, high and hot, beat down on the pavements and lit the lime-coloured leaves on the trees, filtering their branches with a white light. Beneath the trees, shadows danced. A faint smell of tar that had been softened by the sun and was pitted with dents drifted from the road. The heat began to stain Maryssa's pale face, and damp tendrils curled about her forehead. She'd not eaten since the evening before, but was not hungry despite the tantalising smell of hot bagels from the delicatessen.

Except for the fruiterer, the shops were shut down, curled into themselves, part of the quiet lassitude that comes with Sundays. The jeweller's shop display was stripped, showing empty shelves sprinkled with sequins and lined with black satin. Uninterested, she passed the display of clothes in the dress shop windows and crossed the street where Daniel lived, glancing up at his flat. She wondered briefly whether he was at home. A feeling of numbness engulfed her. She walked on quickly to the small red-brick building where Esther lived.

The front room was used as a teaching studio during the week, but today, despite piles of books and papers on the tables and chairs, peace pervaded the crowded space. The scent from a bowl of full blown roses, their petals starting to fall, mingled with the flowery perfume that was Esther's. She was sitting on a sofa that was covered in faded red velvet, leaning against old green velvet cushions.

A white crochet cloth covered the table and a shabby Persian covered the scratched floors. The room had a sense of grace and worn beauty, much like the woman who was drinking tea from a flowered bone china teacup. Esther, with her pale blonde hair fluffed, her creamy skin, the aristocratic angle of her head, her imposing bosom, sat with her heavy shapely smooth white legs crossed and her sandals revealing crimson toenails.

Her kiss, the taking of Maryssa's hand in hers, the glow of stones from her rings, filled Maryssa with comfort as she sank against the caressing cushions. Esther had been her speech teacher from when she was a child and she became Esther's star pupil. Gifted. Esther called her gifted.

Maryssa decided she would not tell her what had happened the night before. She felt soiled. She should never have gone out with David. She was surprised that he'd assumed to take liberties with her. She searched her conscience. Had she behaved inappropriately? Had she played a part in causing that dreadful episode? Perhaps he'd misinterpreted her friendliness. Perhaps she'd smiled too much. Again she worried about what he'd tell his friends, perhaps not even tell the truth, perhaps make out that she'd flirted with him, that they'd had a good time together. Perhaps he would tell that to Daniel. What would Daniel think?

A block of sunlight hung with dust motes was cast across the room. Maryssa was overcome with tiredness. She forced herself to be with Esther, to hear her voice, to watch her expressive dark eyes. She wanted the warmth that flowed from this woman, her mother's best friend, her friend, her teacher.

She sipped hot tea and asked, 'Auntie Esther, tell me what happened to my parents' first child. I know he died suddenly but they never spoke about him. I've never really known what happened…'

Betty, half-crazed, runs into the cold dawn. The moon, thin as tissue paper, stares down at her from an emptied sky. The street is asleep, its windows blinkered. Her feet fly over the stones, their sharp edges cutting her soles. But she feels nothing. She's drenched with perspiration and milk drips from her engorged breasts. Her face is pale and twisted with anguish.

She calls out, 'Oh God! Oh God! No God! NO!' Her mind is ringed in a bright flame as she bangs with clenched fists on Esther's door and cries, 'Esther! Esther! Let me in! PLEASE! Let me in!'

Victor, Esther's husband, opens the door. He looks confused. He rubs his bare barrelled chest. 'Bet? What is it? What's going on?'

She pushes past him crying, and sinks to the floor of their bedroom. Victor lifts her like a child and places her on the bed next to Esther.

'For God's sake! Betty!' Esther pushes herself onto her elbows, her face creased with sleep. 'What is it, darling? What's wrong? What on earth has happened?'

'Esther, my baby's dead. He died…'

'What? What are you saying?'

'He's dead. He was sick last night. Very sick. We called the doctor. He said to give him medicine. Said he'd be OK in the morning. We put him to sleep but he never woke for his next feed. When we went to look, we could see he wasn't breathing. He was dead. Our baby's dead.'

The death notice said gastroenteritis. Not diarrhoea. Not what the doctor had diagnosed.

'Diarrhoea,' he'd told them. 'Nothing to panic about. Get this script. Start the drops tonight. Don't worry. He'll be OK. I'll call by in the morning to have another look at him.'

But when morning came, it was too late. Too late to make the urgent call. Too late to send the child to hospital. Too late to administer a drip.

He'd shaken his head and stared at the tortured young father, at the uncomprehending young mother who stared back at him, silent, wordless.

As the day wears on, an overwhelming grief envelops Ellis. He paces through the flat and, together with his pain, there is anger that erupts in terrible curses against the doctor. Every possible curse is cast upon him. Not only curses but threats. He threatens to get him! To get a gang onto him! That murderer! That bastard! 'I'll kill him! With my bare hands! I'll choke the life out of him! That swine! That bastard! He killed my son! He killed my baby!'

In the days that follow, they can do little but hold each other and cry. For Betty, it seems that her tears will never end, that she will weep forever. They cry in the spring days of November, in the heat of summer. They wake in the night from their shallow, uneasy sleep and, in the white shafts of moonlight, they wipe the tears from each other's faces.

Then, as time passes, and with the expectancy of another child, Maryssa,

Esther looked at her with dark warm eyes.

'You were born on the day the baby died, exactly one year later,'
she said softly.

Daniel had sat at the window in the dark and looked into the black sky, at the pinpricks of stars, at the moon that hung low and yellow. He'd watched a cat slink along the pavement, become a sphinx, then spring into a bush on the side of the road. He waited for it to reappear but it was gone. He lay down for a while, then, unable to sleep, drank some water and switched on his lamp.

He was disturbed by images of David and Maryssa, and worried about the impression he'd given of her and the advantage David might have taken of her. Maryssa was a sensitive person. She was refined. She was respectable. He'd given the wrong message. For his own benefit, he'd led his friends to believe that she was compliant and willing. The conversation he'd had with them implied that she was easy – a good-time girl. He was angry with himself for giving that impression and uncomfortable with one of his friends taking Maryssa out. He resolved to see David the next day, after his ward rounds. He needed to tell him that Maryssa was his girlfriend. That he was serious about her. That he didn't want any of the other guys around her, dating her.

The morning at the hospital never seemed to come to an end. He'd checked the time repeatedly and was agitated by the time he arrived at the hotel. He sat in his car for a while to regain his composure, needing to appear casual, unconcerned.

David was in the foyer and he steered him to a corner seat in the lounge.

'Hey, Davey,' he smiled. 'How's it going? How're things?'

'Howz't, Dan. OK. All OK. How's with you?'

'Ja. OK. Long day. Pleased it's over. So. How's everything going?'

'Like I said. All OK.'

'That's good. I came looking for you last night. Thought we'd do a movie.'

'I was out.'

'I know. Where were you?'

'Last night? Where was I last night? Last night I was on a date.'

'With who?'

David looked at Daniel quizzically. 'Why do you ask?'

'Were you with Maryssa?'

'I was.'

'And. How was it? How did it go?'

'How did what go?'

'How did the date go?'

'The date? It was OK.'

'How did you and Maryssa go?'

'OK. As I said – it was OK.'

'Hey, Davey. Stop playing games. You know what I'm asking. How did you make out?' Daniel began to feel tense. He was angry with David, frustrated with his responses, but he knew he had to keep the conversation light, appear to make the outcome inconsequential. He needed to appear unconcerned.

David, on the other hand, was not sure what he wanted to share with Daniel. It had been an unpleasant evening. Something he preferred to forget. He sat silently, thinking. What he should say? How would he describe the evening so that he would not come out in a bad light? He'd behaved very badly. He knew that. He was concerned what Maryssa might say about him. Of course, if she did talk, he would deny it. Tell them she was exaggerating. Creating a big drama over nothing. They'd believe him before her. Why would they listen to her? All those thoughts flew through his head.

'How did I make out? With Maryssa?'

'Ja. You know what I'm talking about? How far did you guys go?'

'How far did we go?' David leaned towards Daniel, suddenly becoming intense. 'You're asking me if I made out with her. If I got anywhere with her. My *boet*! I never got to first base. Never even held her hand. Akshully, I found the whole evening a helluva bore.

A total waste of time. Akshully, I don't even think she's that good-looking. Quite frankly, I can't make out what you see in her. She does nothing for me. For my part, I wouldn't bother to go there again. She's definitely not for me.' Then David asked, 'Why are you so interested, Dan? Didn't you say it's all for one and one for all? That you weren't that linked in any more?'

Daniel did not respond. With a huge sense of relief, he leaned back in his seat, an image of Maryssa in his mind. He saw her smile, the golden lights of her eyes. Maryssa stirred him like no other. She'd entered into his inner sanctum, his soul. His feelings for her were overwhelming, profound.

He smiled his thin smile, looked at David with a gentle expression on his face and said quietly, 'Did I say that? Is that what I said?'

'So. Where are you going now?'

'Out.'

'Out! Out! You're going out!'

'That's what I said. Out.'

'You're always going out! You know what, Joe, you had no right to get married. You got no right to be a father. You don't know what it means to have a wife. To have children. You're always running. Where are you running? Do I know? Do you tell me? Out! That's what you tell me. Out!'

'I'm going to play cards. With the boys.'

'Cards? You mean poker. With money. You play with money. I know. But what about me? What about the kids? You got three beautiful kids. Why don't you stay home? Spend time with them? Ask them how was their day? How is their schoolwork? You don't know about their schoolwork. You don't ask them. You're not interested. You're always want to go away from us…'

'Oh, shuddup. I told you, I'm playing cards. It's my card night.'

'Every night's your card night!'

'So what! You think it's such a joy to be home with you? You think you're such wonderful company? Always nagging. Always going on about something. Sure I go out. To get away from you.'

'Listen here, Joe. Listen to me good. Either you married or you not married. Either you committed to us or you not committed to us. That's what a marriage is. Commitment. But you don't know what that means. You were never committed. Not from day one! You always had your eye somewhere else. Other husbands spend time with their wives. They spend time with their children. But you! Never! The kids don't know what it means to have a real father. Look at Daniel. Such a lovely boy. When does he see you? You're never here. Always playing poker, and God knows what else. Maybe you with other women?'

'Listen here. Shut your trap. I've had enough of you. I'm going out. Like I said, there's no joy being in this place. It's bladdy miserable here. What should I be here for? For you? Big deal! To spend time with you? In your wonderful company? But you are right in one thing. You're absolutely right. I'm not committed to this marriage. I'm definitely not committed to all this shit! Why the hell should I be?'

'Joe, just listen to you…all this and right in front of your son.'

'So what! Let him know. What are we bluffing for? He should know. They should all know. I'm not committed to you. I'm not committed to them. In fact, the sooner this comes to an end, the better.'

The boy sat with downcast eyes. His crisp dark curls were twisted between his fingers. He tried not to listen, tried to read his book but his vision was blurred and through his tears he heard, over and over again, 'I'm not committed! I'm not committed!'

He remembered that evening as though it was yesterday.

He thought about the word, committed. He thought about its implications. He recalled the terrible relationship of his parents – his mother's expectations of their marriage, his father running away from it. Marriage was a serious business. Relationships meant commitment. Relationships sometimes led to marriage.

Daniel thought about it. He thought about the implications of a serious committed relationship with Maryssa. Again he felt that he was not ready for it. He resolved to not tell David that Maryssa was his girlfriend. 'Why should I tell him how I feel?' he thought. 'Who knows? I'll probably change my mind about her. In a year or two, she may be out of my life. In any case, it's none of David's business what my involvement with Maryssa is. The truth is, I don't want to be committed to her. I don't want to be committed to anyone.'

The sun was high and burning in a seamless blue sky when Maryssa left Esther's building. She walked along the hot and airless Main Road, her mind filled with thoughts of the brother she never knew, and of the pain her parents had gone through from losing him. Esther said that was when her father started his drinking. She said that from that time her mother was always taking pills. Maryssa thought how the baby's death had changed their lives, had changed them from the people they were before their loss, had changed them from the people they might have become.

They'd never spoken of their first child. There were no photographs, no mementoes. She remembered that her mother had given all the baby clothes away. This fragment of information came from a discussion she'd once heard. Someone had asked. Her mother had answered, No, she'd kept nothing. Maryssa wondered if they'd ever visited the little grave. She wondered where he was buried. She knew nothing of him other than that she was named after him, that her initials were the same as his.

She turned into London Road. Daniel was there, leaning against his car, his long legs crossed, his arms folded, his eyes shaded in dark glasses. He smiled and in a rush her thoughts changed to him, to David, to the night before. Uneasy, unsmiling, she walked towards him, wanting him to take off his sun glasses, wanting to see the expression in his eyes. Daniel's eyes reflected what he thought. Did he know about her date with David? Had he spoken to him?

'Hi.'

'Hello.'

'Where've you been?'

'To visit someone.'

'I was here last night, and I phoned. Did Leech tell you?'

'Yes, I got the messages.'

'I've had a helluva week. I've been flat out.'

They faced each other in silence.

Then Maryssa asked, 'Have you seen David?'

'Ja. I saw him…'

'Did he say anything? I mean, did he say anything about me?'

'Like what?'

'I went out with him last night. He took me to see a play.'

'Oh. Was it good?'

'It was OK.' She could not see his eyes.

'He mentioned your date. Didn't have much to say about it…'

'If I'd known you were coming last night, I would never have gone out with him.'

'Don't worry about it. You're entitled to go out with whoever you want.'

'I know that. But he's your friend. It wasn't right of me to accept, and I certainly won't go out with him again.' She turned away and the terrible feelings she'd woken with that morning came flooding back.

He removed his sunglasses. His eyes were warm. 'Hey, Maryssa. Forget it. It's not a big deal. Just a date. Look. It's a beautiful day. Why don't you grab your cossie and come with me to the beach?'

'Not Clifton,' she said quickly. 'I don't feel like that big crowd.'

'OK with me. We can go to Llandudno. Would you like to go there?'

'Ja. That'll be OK.'

He noticed that her voice was flat, that her face remained expressionless. 'I'll wait for you. Go get your stuff.'

The sun played with her hair as she walked away, lighting it in red and gold. He thought of his carelessness and, for a moment, felt guilty. It was his fault. He was to blame. He knew that he had caused her this upset. He knew that she did not deserve it.

They drove along the curves of the coast. The cliffs were high and dense on one side of the road, and, on the other side, fell sharply away to the sea. The water danced with refracted light, and in the distance the ocean flowed towards the horizon in fluid shades of turquoise and blue. In front of them, Bakoven stretched on a promontory into the surf, its houses perched on the rocks, facing endless space.

Maryssa said, 'Look at those gorgeous houses! Right there. In the middle of all that sea. Can you just imagine how amazing it would be to live in one of those…'

'I know someone who did,' Daniel said. 'I know a couple who saved for years to buy one of those. That was their dream.'

'Did their dream come true?'

'It certainly did. And it turned into a nightmare.'

'Why?'

'They moved in. Great excitement. Then. One year later, they moved out.'

'What happened?'

'They couldn't sleep. The sound of the surf. The waves against the rocks. Day and night. Kept them awake. None of them could sleep. It was like Chinese torture. They absolutely hated it. Got out as soon as they could. Moved to Constantia…'

'Shows you. Who would have thought of that? I mean, it looks fantastic.'

'What looks fantastic often isn't all that fantastic.'

'Right…' She turned to look at him. 'You're right…' Again the silence. 'Daniel.' Her voice was small and she faced the passing cliffs. 'I had a bad experience with David…'

He watched the road. 'What?'

'He tried to force himself on me. After the play, he took me to Green Point. He parked there and he tried to…'

Daniel was silent. He was alert. He needed to be careful. Quietly he said, 'Did he? Doesn't sound like the sort of thing David would do.'

'Well, he did. It was terrible. I really had a struggle. He forced himself onto me. I tried to push him off but he was too strong. I was so desperate I tried to open the car door. I wanted to run away, to run back to the hotel… I was frantic. He only stopped because there was another car parked there and they were looking at us…'

'David did that?' Daniel felt anger rise within him.

'He did. I was so upset…'

He parked the car and took her hand in his. It felt small and dry. He kissed her fingers and smelled her perfume. 'That's very bad,' he said softly. 'I'm sorry you had to go through that. He shouldn't have done that.'

'I know. I was very upset. I still am. I've never had that happen to me. This is the first time someone has tried to force themselves on me… I was actually frightened of him.'

'I can understand. No guy should behave in that way.'

Maryssa's eyes filled with tears.

He put his arm around her. 'Come.' He held her close, kissed her hair. 'Try not to think about it. Try to put it out of your mind. Grab your things. Come with me. I've got something to show you…'

The rock is hidden except from the sea. It is closed on three sides by massive boulders that fold against each other to form an almost impenetrable barrier. Daniel knows its secret entrance, the small spaces, the way through.

The rock is smooth and flat, supported by a ragged cliff that is eternally lashed by the tireless sea. When the sea is at its most passionate, the crevices of its underbelly are invaded by pounding surf. After the storms, when the passion subsides, when the sea is still, the rock, too, is at rest, its cracks filled with soft white salty loam.

'It's where I come to be quiet,' Daniel said, facing the sea, the pale horizon. His dark hair, his dark eyes, his chiselled profile, were etched against a sun-bleached boulder. He turned to her and smiled. 'I've brought you to my secret place.'

There was a sense of secrecy here, a sealed in space, private and isolated.

'It reminds me of him,' Maryssa thought. 'Hidden. Secretive. Hard to penetrate.' She recalled the times they'd spent together, the intimate moments when she knew that it was only her that he wanted. She remembered the times she'd waited for him to tell her, to say with words what he'd showed her with the warmth of his eyes, with the passion of his body. 'He knows I love him, but how does he feel? Sometimes I think he does have feelings for me, then he moves away, becomes a stranger.'

'Ted liked places like this,' she said softly. 'Hidden places. Secret places. Places where there's water.'

'I was thinking about him the other day. Hard to believe that he's no longer around. I can't imagine Jo'burg without him.'

'Neither can I. We used to spend a lot of time together. He was always there. Always kind. Always helpful. He taught me to drive. In his little three-wheeled buggy. The doors wouldn't open. They were stuck. We had to climb over them to get in and out, and sometimes I was in high heels and a tight skirt...' She smiled shyly.

Daniel took her hand and pressed the tips of his fingers against hers. A striped shadow in the shape of a pyramid fell onto the rock.

'He liked you,' he said. 'A lot. He spoke very highly of you. Did you know that?'

'No, I didn't. We were good friends. We used to have fun together.'

'You never had a relationship?'

'No. We liked each other and we liked being together. But that's all there was...'

'Did he ever have a girlfriend? Do you know if he was ever involved with anyone?'

'Not that I know of. He was a solitary kind of guy. Didn't seem to mind spending time on his own. I don't know of any girl that he dated. Come to think of it, I think I was the only girl he spent time with.'

'He was very protective of you. But more than that – I think he fancied you. In a big way. He was just not up to making the right moves...'

'Well, maybe he sensed that I never fancied him. Not in that way. You know, not in a physical way. But I really liked him as a person. He was a wonderful guy.'

'He was. A great guy. Really. One in a million...'

Maryssa lay on the rock. It was smooth and warm against her back. She recalled lying on another rock.

She said, 'He took us to a pool once, a big black pool on the top of a mountain in the Magaliesberg. In a way, it reminds me of this place. Lots of sky, lots of quiet, the air still...like a huge natural open cathedral, it almost felt like a place of worship.' But, she thought, that sense of something else, something intangible, that exquisite feeling she'd experienced in that space with Ted, she did not feel in this hidden place of boulders.

He traced her profile gently with one finger, and then her jawline.

She closed her eyes. The blue sea and sky became navy behind her lids. He moved his finger over the outline of her lips, touched her thickly fringed eyelids with his lips.

The sun had coloured her skin in rose and milky brown. He stroked her smooth shoulders, her smooth arms.

'Dan?' She looked at him.

'I'm examining you. Do you mind?'

She closed her eyes against the glare. 'As a doctor?'

'No. Not as a doctor…'

'And what are you finding?'

'I'll let you know… I've got a way to go…'

The sun was warm, the air soft, still, the sea quiet. Daniel's hands were gentle as he stroked her calves. He held her foot in his palm, and then the other.

Maryssa was both soothed and stimulated by his touch, and, as he stretched beside her leaning on his elbows, his face close to hers, she ran her fingers through his hair, looked at him, smiled and asked, 'Well? What's the verdict?'

'Almost perfect.'

'Almost?'

'Yes. You've got a crooked toe.'

She laughed. 'That's my only imperfection?'

'I think so… Do you want me to look further?'

'You know what the rest of me looks like. You've seen me. All of me…'

'I want to see all of you again. Do you mind?'

'Dan…'

They looked deeply into each other's eyes, his dark intense gaze meeting the tawny lights of hers. He touched the corner of her mouth. She turned to kiss his finger, then, blushing, looked away as he slipped the straps of her bathing suit from her shoulders. Softly he kissed her breasts.

She took his head in her hands.

In that secret place among the boulders, they explored the secret places of each other and were filled with desire and wanting, with an overwhelming need to come together as they had never been before. In that hidden place, they discovered what had been hidden from them – what had previously been withheld. As the sea rose and swelled, as the waves welled, so did their need for each other rise in waves of desire. They whispered each other's names, told each other what they needed, what to do, what they wanted. The forces within them exploded with desire and wanting. Unbounded and primitive, they moved in perfect rhythm until they reached the pinnacle of their love.

Maryssa cried out as she clung to Daniel. With her tears came a sensation she had never experienced before, amazing waves of ecstatic bliss. 'I love you, Daniel,' Maryssa whispered. 'I really do love you.'

Daniel lay with his head on her chest, their legs entwined, her arms around his waist. The sun had moved, its rays oblique. A breeze from the ocean played on the sea, stirring its smooth surface. In the warm balm of the afternoon, in the circle of her arms, against the softness of her, Daniel closed his eyes. They could feel their hearts beat, their breathing becoming quiet and shallow.

Maryssa was filled with bliss and joy and contentment. She stroked Daniel's forehead, thought how much she loved this man, how she wanted this moment to go on and on, how she wanted to be with him forever.

In the enclosure of boulders, on the smooth warm rock, the high clear sky above them, they fell asleep holding each other, perfectly together.

They woke to an orange sun in a stained and flaming sky. It was cooler now and Maryssa shivered as she pulled on her clothes. Daniel sat holding his knees looking at the horizon, at the pinks and mauves and reds, at the smouldering disc of sun at it started to dip into the ocean.

'Isn't that something?' his voice said, almost to himself.

She touched his shoulder. He turned to her and they kissed.

'You should get dressed,' she smiled. 'It's getting cold…'

He took her hand, turned it over and kissed her palm. 'You OK?' he asked.

'Yes.'

He watched her face as he dressed. 'It was good. Wasn't it?'

She smiled and kissed him. 'Wonderful. Really wonderful.'

It was when he bent to tie his shoelaces that he saw the stain. He stared down at it and said, 'What's that?' He touched it then looked at her. 'It's blood. Did you cut yourself?'

'No.'

Daniel was quiet for a moment, then asked, 'Are you menstruating?'

'No, I'm not…'

'So what's that?'

Maryssa's face suffused with bright colour. She avoided his eyes and looked out at the reddened sky, at the cold sea. 'I'm not sure…'

'Maryssa. Look at me. Tell me. Was this your first time?'

She turned to him apprehensively. 'Yes,' she answered quietly. 'It was…'

'The first time you've had intercourse?'

'Yes. This is the first time.'

'So you were a virgin?'

'Are you surprised?'

'I don't know. I, uh, I somehow thought…'

'Thought what?'

'I never thought I'd be the first one with you. To tell the truth, had I known, I wouldn't have done it. I wouldn't have wanted to take that from you.'

'It was my decision. I wanted you to be the one. I'd always hoped to be a virgin when I got married, to keep myself for my husband. But I'm pleased it was you. Because I love you… You know I love you…'

Daniel's face hardened. 'I can't marry you,' he said quickly. 'You realise that. Marriage is out. I've got a lot to do. I've got to specialise…'

'I know. But maybe in the future, when you've done what you need to do…'

'There is no future, Maryssa. For me, there's only now. Only what I need to do right now. There is no future for us.'

'Are you saying that none of this means anything to you? That I mean nothing to you?'

He turned away. She saw his profile outlined against the darkening sky. It was harsh and unsmiling. 'I'm saying that for us there is no future.'

'But don't you feel anything for me? All this time we've been together? Has it meant nothing to you? Do I mean nothing to you?'

'Maryssa.' His voice was strained. 'Leave it alone. I don't want to talk about it. Just leave it. Please. Take your things. We need to go.'

The light was fading as they left the beach. The dusk was grey and oppressive. Cliffs loomed over them, cragged and jagged, in dark giant shadows. The sea seemed flat and oily.

Maryssa stared ahead, her arms folded tightly around her slight form. Numbness overcame her. She was chilled. She shivered. Remembering the bloodstain on the rock, she tried to associate with it, relate it to her body. She wondered how it had happened, where it came from. 'Something was penetrated. Something must have been torn. My virginity's gone…' she thought, felt tears welling in her eyes and brushed them away with the back of her hand.

Her perfume, her woman smell, filtered the small space. This was what had always reminded Daniel of her. This was what lingered. It was the embodiment of her. It remained with him, as though she was still with him, still beside him. Now, driving back with his hands tightly holding the wheel, with his jaw clenched and his lips a thin line, for the first time, he was unaware of it.

He was angry with himself. He'd been careless. Caught up in the moment. He should have worn protection. He'd come inside her. Perhaps he should tell her to douche, to wash herself, to try and rid herself of his sperm. What if she should fall pregnant? He certainly couldn't marry her. He was not in a position to marry anyone.

Feeling tense and ill at ease, he drove faster than he should have, taking the curves sharply, harshly applying the brakes, causing the car to jolt, focusing fixedly on the road.

The silence between them was like a wall. There was a palpable feeling of separation, an irreparable division of one entity into two. A break had taken place, just as Maryssa had been broken. It could not be fixed. It could not be mended.

The car swung into London Road, taking the corner too close to the curb. Someone shouted out in protest. Daniel pulled up abruptly at the entrance to the annexe. Maryssa picked up her bag, opened the door and swung her legs out onto the pavement.

'Maryssa, wait. I'll see you in.' Daniel opened his side of the car.

'Please don't,' she answered coldly. 'I really don't want you to.' She stood slim and stiff against the street light, then bent down to face him. Looking at him directly and without expression. she said slowly and deliberately, 'This is goodbye. Daniel. I don't want to see you. Not ever again.'

Daniel had driven home that evening feeling agitated and upset. Maryssa was emphatic in her dismissal of him and in ending their relationship. In some ways, he was relieved that it was over. He could now focus fully on his future. He could also rid himself of those persistent feelings about her, let them dissipate and, finally, hopefully, disappear. After all, she was just a girl – among many girls.

He'd worried about the unprotected sex they shared and hoped that there would be no complications from that. In that event, he'd formulated a plan. He had a friend who knew a friend who did abortions. If the worst happened, he would insist on that. He would not marry her. She would have to end the pregnancy.

He stayed away from the hotel, not wanting to see her, pleased with each day that passed without contact from her. He estimated when she should have her period and, with each passing week, was relieved and hopeful that all was well, that no unfortunate mistake had been made.

The end of the year was a busy time at the hospital. Accidents, fights and knifings took place with increasing regularity as Christmas loomed, as people drank more, used their bonuses to buy beer and cheap wines. The emergency department was filled with patients and Daniel offered to help after he'd done his ward rounds and assisted with surgeries. The extra work filled his evenings, and when he drove home he was often exhausted.

He was too tired to know that summer was everywhere. The days were glorious, full of golden sunshine, unblemished skies, sparkling white tipped waves that crashed on both sides of the peninsula. Trees were thickly green and garden perfumes permeated the air. There was a constant drone of bees, the raucous calls of seagulls, the hoot of an owl in the night. And in the night skies, stars burnished bright and the moon rode high and proud, throwing a white path across the seas.

The city was filled with visitors from the north, sunburnt, in shorts, packing into restaurants, cramming the beaches, smelling of tanning oils and Nivea cream. Crowds of excited young people chatted and laughed on street corners. It was the season for the city. The city was on heat.

'You should go the beach, Daniel,' his mother said on a Sunday morning. 'You could do with a bit of sun. It's a beautiful day...'

Daniel chewed a bagel, his face half hidden by a newspaper. 'Maybe I will,' he mumbled.

She answered a telephone call and he heard her say, 'Oh. Well, that's very nice. As you say, it's about time he settled down. Thirty-two? And she's only twenty? Quite a big age difference. Well. Mazel tov. All the best. When? On the twenty-second of next month? Yes. Of course. I'd love to. I always enjoy watching you play. I'll ask Daniel.'

To Daniel, she said, 'That was Ella. She offered me two comps for her concert at the City Hall next month. She's playing Beethoven. Maybe you'd like to come with me?'

'Maybe I will. She's a good pianist.'

'She is good. But she always gets the same crit in the paper – technically brilliant but very little emotion. Anyway, I don't care what they say. I enjoy her playing.'

'What was the mazel tov for?'

'They've got an engagement in their family...'

'Who got engaged?'

'Her brother-in-law. Keith. To a Jo'burg girl. Much younger than him.'

'Well, she's onto a good wicket. Rich family. They must own half of Cape Town.'

'Yes. She's certainly made a good match for herself.' She looked at him quizzically. 'That's what you should do, Daniel. I'm not saying marry for money. But marry where money is. It makes life a lot easier.'

'Ma, please don't talk to me about marriage. Nothing, at this stage, could be further from my mind.'

'I know. I know. I'm just saying. When the time comes, there's no harm in marrying where there's a bit of money...'

'OK. I've heard what you've said. I'll marry for money. But right now, I'm off to the beach.'

It was the first time he'd travelled along the cliff since that day with Maryssa. The road was quiet and he felt calm. He did not miss Maryssa. He also told himself that he would not be visiting the rock again. He would not miss the rock. But when he parked his car high above Clifton, he did glance up the coastline towards Llandudno. In the distance, he could see the pale outline of the boulders.

Far below him, the beach was filled with beach goers. The water, brilliantly caught in the rays of the sun, danced and sparkled, and the waves flowed majestically, crowned in white foam. With his towel over his shoulder, Daniel walked down the flights of stone and sandy steps, looking forward to being there, among the people and with his friends. He wondered if he would see Maryssa. He usually felt her presence, but today he had no sensation, no warning sign that she might be on the beach.

David Finkelstein was the first to see him. 'Hey, Danny! Howzit! Long time no see...'

'Hi.' Daniel grinned.

'Danny, my boy! What's with you? You disappeared! You haven't been near or by the hotel for weeks. The guys were saying, "What's happened to Daniel?"'

'You're right, Finks. I have been scarce. I've been busy. I've had a fortune of work to get through.'

'No excuse. A guy always makes time to connect with his friends.' David squinted against the sun. 'We thought maybe you were avoiding us...'

'Why would I do that?'

'Who knows?' David wouldn't let it go. 'Well, maybe it wasn't us you were avoiding...'

'How do you mean?' Daniel's dark glasses hid the expression in his eyes.

'Well, Maryssa. It seems like maybe it was Maryssa. It seems like it's all over for the two of you...'

Daniel tried to avoid answering him. He hedged. 'You're right. I haven't been round for a while.'

'Ja. We noticed…' David paused. 'We also noticed that she's got a huge rock on her finger.'

'Who?'

'Maryssa. She's engaged.'

'Engaged?'

'Ja. She got engaged. A couple of days ago.'

'To who?'

'Keith Davidoff. You know, from Davidoff Developers. The builders…'

'Maryssa's engaged to him?'

'That's right. He's the guy.'

There was a silence. David looked down and awkwardly moved his foot in the sand.

'So,' Daniel's voice was quiet, his tone measured. 'Maryssa's got herself engaged…'

David watched his friend closely. 'You aw'right, buddy?'

Daniel was silent.

'Daniel? You OK?'

'Ja…'

David persisted. 'Hey, Dan. Listen. We've been friends for a long time. Tell me. What happened with you two? I mean… I thought… We all thought… You two were an item, you know… Kind of made for each other…'

Daniel took off his glasses. Although his voice was calm, his eyes were dark with pain. 'We broke up a few weeks ago. That's all there is to it.' And then he said, 'Jesus. It's bladdy hot. I think I'll go and cool down.'

He dropped his towel onto the sand and ran towards the sea.

He was not sure how the rest of the day passed. There was the crush of the crowd, the murmur of voices, laughter, someone calling his name. He vaguely recalled promising to be somewhere, at someone's house, but afterwards could not recall the details of that arrangement or who the person was.

He walked up the many steps to the parking lot without registering the heat and the strenuous climb, wiped his face with his towel and resolved to go to the hotel to see her. But she wasn't there and he left no message. He drove to Green Point, to the parking lot that lovers used in moonlight, agitated and out of touch with what was happening around him.

The sun burned in the sky, the waves were high and sullen. In the distance, was the grim outline of Robben Island. A doctor from the hospital had been sent there a few months before to contain an outbreak of a particularly bad strain of influenza. He told them it was an ugly place – no waving palms, no pristine beaches. Mainly rock. A growth of tough shrubs. Plenty of *dassies*.* There was no fresh water on the island, no natural spring. Water had to be shipped in every day.

They asked him about the prisoners, about Nelson Mandela. Had he seen him? He had. He'd been into his cell.

'What's he like?' they asked.

'Imposing. He has a definite aura about him. Commands respect without demanding it.' he replied. 'A refined guy…a gentleman…'

'What do they do, these prisoners?'

'They work in a lime pit. All day. Chipping lime.' He showed them a lump of limestone he'd brought back as a memento. It was now a paperweight. 'The only good thing about that place is the view,' he said. 'Table Mountain looks amazing from there, and the dockyard with all the ships is beautiful. At night, the lights are like a fairyland. Really stunning.'

'Do any of the prisoners try to escape? Swim away from the island?'

He told them that there had been many attempts, but no one had succeeded. They drowned in the treacherous sea, in powerful whirlpools and strong rips, in the malevolent Cape rollers. The guards never pursued the escapees. They let them go. They knew they would not reach the other side.

* wild rabbits

Someone said, 'Terrible punishment for them. Those guys'll be there forever.'

Someone else said, 'Well, they were found guilty of treason. Trying to overthrow the Nats. They're lucky to be alive. Other countries would have hung them.'

Daniel stared at the island. He watched the waves break against the sea wall, the spray shoot above and over the wall in drifts of white foam. On the horizon, dark clouds accumulated. The seagulls were sullen, the sign of a storm. He remembered how he and Maryssa had watched the buck come down to the fence from the mountain heights when a storm was brewing.

He tried to calm his thoughts, to get his mind in order. He had to see her. They had to talk. In the weeks that had passed, he'd remembered her as she'd always been, in her small room, waiting for him. He'd thought that, if he wanted to, he'd only need to reach out to take her hand.

This new situation was foreign to him. He felt immensely hurt and threatened. He had a profound sense of loss, a great gaping wound within him that was almost a physical pain. His mind was a whirlwind. He told himself that he could not accept this, that he could not leave this be. He had to see her.

He had to have her back.

For the first time, he realised how much he loved her. He could not imagine his life without her. She was an integral part of who he was. He now knew this. It was quite clear to him that he now had to put all else aside, his studies, his plans, his future, because, without her, there was no future.

Of course he would marry her. Immediately. He'd make it work. Together they would move forward. She would come with him to England. She would be at his side. That was what he wanted. He knew now that that was all he wanted. Her beside him every day. Sharing every aspect of his life.

He needed Maryssa with him always.

The clouds moved quickly. There was a blinding crack of lightning, the ominous sound of thunder, ferocious warnings of the approaching storm.

Robben Island was a dark uneven shadow in the dark sea. He thought of the prisoners who would now be locked their cells. 'Will they really be there forever?' he thought fleetingly.

The heavens answered with rapiers of vicious lightning and furious rumbles of thunder. Then down in great torrents came the unstoppable black rain.

Daniel resolved to see Maryssa that evening. He drove to the hotel again and knocked on her door. He tried the handle. The door was locked. He waited then knocked again. There was no response.

He went home, showered and changed his clothes. Thankfully, his mother was out. Daniel did not want to speak to anyone, least of all her. She had a way of knowing his mood without even looking at him, and he did not want her asking questions.

He tried to phone Maryssa. Leech said she was out. He left no message. Pacing around the flat, he became uneasy and decided to drive to the hospital. There were patients he wanted to see, young boys who'd been very unwell the week before. His work controlled him, gave him a sense of purpose and balance. Yes, he resolved, he'd go and check those two youngsters out. See how they were doing.

The rain was less intense as he drove along the highway. He felt strangely light, as though he'd already resolved the situation with Maryssa. But he needed to concentrate on his driving. Two drivers had hooted at him disapprovingly as he swung out of lanes without checking his rear-view mirror. Daniel was being reckless, not aware of the blurred windows, the wet roads, other cars.

He reached the hospital, swung into the parking area and immediately phoned the hotel from a public call box.

'No,' said Leech. 'Mizz Klein's not back yet, doctor, sir.'

His rounds took longer than expected. He held an informal consultation with one of the senior doctors whom he met unexpectedly and gratefully absorbed the advice of this man, for whom he had high regard.

By the time he reached the hotel, it was after nine o'clock. The rain had cleared and there was a fresh clean feel in the air. Trees sparkled under the street lights and the gutters ran strongly with streams of gushing water.

He knocked on her door.

'Who is it?' she called.

Daniel's heart raced. 'Daniel.'

She opened the door.

'Hi.' He smiled but he felt awkward. It seemed so long since he'd last seen her.

'What are you doing here?'

'I need to see you. May I come in?'

She did not open the door further. 'What about?'

'I can't talk here, in the passageway…'

She studied his face for a few moments. 'I'm really busy. Why can't you tell me what you want?'

'Maryssa. Please. I need to talk to you. Please let me in.'

He entered the small room that looked smaller with the curtains drawn. But there was her perfume, light and flowery and heartbreakingly familiar. She stood facing him, her face golden under the dull electric light, her hair thick and lustrous. He thought that she had never she looked more beautiful.

'Maryssa.' He reached out to her but she backed away. 'You're looking great,' he said quietly.

'Thanks. What is it, Daniel? Why are you here?'

'I've come because I heard that you're engaged…'

She was silent.

'Is it true? Are you engaged?'

She looked at him in that direct way that she had, almost as though she was looking through him. 'I am,' she answered.

'You can't be serious?'

'Of course I'm serious.'

'But it's only been a few weeks since we broke up. How could you have got engaged so soon after we stopped seeing each other?'

She smiled, but it wasn't her smile. 'These things don't take long when everything is right.'

'How can everything be right when just a few weeks ago you were in love with me?'

She turned away. Her profile was in shadow. She answered very softly. 'Things change. I've changed. I've met a wonderful man and I'm very happy with him.'

'What you're saying doesn't make sense to me. Falling in and out of love, then back in love with someone else so quickly just doesn't happen. It can't. There's too much involved emotionally. It's just not possible to switch like that.'

'Well, it did happen. And, as I said, I'm very happy with him.'

'Maryssa, listen to me. I'm here to tell you you're making the mistake of your life. You shouldn't marry this guy, whoever he is. You should be marrying me. I love you. I want to marry you. I want us to be together. Forever. I love you, Maryssa. I love you.'

Maryssa looked at Daniel, at the anguish in his dark eyes, at his gaunt face, hollowed by shadows. She'd never known him to be as exposed as he was, as humble, as serious, as sincere. He said he loved her. He said he wanted her. He wanted to marry her. He said all the words that she'd yearned to hear, all that she'd longed for with every fibre of her being. Daniel had actually come to her to tell her that he loved her.

Her eyes filled with tears. 'Thank you for telling me that you love me. It means a lot to me.' She took his hands gently in her own. 'But I can't marry you. I'm engaged. I'm marrying someone else…'

He tried to interrupt. 'Maryssa, I've told you, you're making a huge mistake.'

She placed her finger on his lips and said, 'Please listen to me. I'm with someone who makes me very happy. He really loves me. He treats me like gold. He makes me feel that I'm the centre of his world. We've made promises to each other. We made plans for our lives together. I would never break my word to him.'

Daniel sank onto the bed. 'I can't believe what you're telling me. He may love you, but I know that you love me. We're made for each other Maryssa. You know that. I'm asking you to marry me. Now. We can get married tomorrow…'

She took his head in her hands, turned his face to her and said, 'Dan, you're not ready to get married. You have a long road ahead. You only want me because you think you've lost me. Please, just listen. You'll get over me. When the right time comes, you'll find someone else. Someone much better than me. A girl from a really good family. Someone with a university degree. Someone who will enhance your life. Who will match you in every way. I'm not right for you. I'm really very ordinary. To tell the truth, I regard myself as lucky to have found someone like Keith.'

'Maryssa, you're wrong. Completely wrong. You and I belong together.'

'Do we? Would it work for us? I don't think it would. We're too much alike. We'd only pull each other down as we've always done. We've not been good for each other. A lot of the time we tortured each other. Why would that change?'

'It would change because I'll change. I'd do everything in my power to make it better for us …'

'Daniel, if it was right, if we were meant to be together, you wouldn't have to do that. When it's right, it flows. Not one or the other has to change, or to work at it. Both just have to be. That's how it is for us now, and that's how it will one day be for you.'

Daniel shook his head. 'No, Maryssa, that's not how it will be. You are the one I want. Only you. I ask you please not to rush into anything. Give it time. Think about what I've said. Give us another chance.'

Maryssa's voice was filled with sadness. 'No, Daniel. I've made my decision. I'm not going back on my word. There's nothing to think about. Nothing more to say.'

She opened the door. 'You need to go now.'

In that small intense space, her voice was barely audible.

It would be ten years before they spoke to each other again. On a perfect evening brilliant with moon and stars, they met in a large house on a hill overlooking the ocean. At night, from the house, the water looked black and impenetrable. This evening, an illuminated liner, as small as a toy, was anchored there, waiting for daybreak to enter the docks.

Outside, limousines lined the wide streets – Porches, Mercedes Benzes, convertible MGs, a Maserati. They gleamed under street lights, each with its own identity, luxurious trappings of the influential and the wealthy.

Inside the house, crystal chandeliers shimmered in the entrance hall, the lounge and dining room. Their doors folded back to create an expansive area furnished with plush silken couches and elegant velvet armchairs, antique tables holding priceless ornaments, and impressive bronze sculptures. A huge French armoire filled one wall. Flowers were everywhere, abundantly arranged in priceless vases, their scents blending with other expensive perfumes in the room.

Dressed in white jackets with red sashes, waiters brought dainty hors d'oeuvre around on silver platters, and champagne was served in glittering cut-glass wine goblets. Classical music filtered softly through the rooms.

The guests grouped, animated, in conversation. They flowed perfectly with their surroundings. Refined, discreet, quietly confident, they drifted through the rooms, greeting each other warmly, talking, laughing, but ever watchful. The women had cultivated the art of conversation, listening carefully, considering their own responses, using the right inflections in their voices and the right expressions on their faces, whether it be a smile, a show of surprise, a nod of approval, while at the very same time assessing in detail what the other was wearing. What make the dress, whether the necklace was a new piece or remodelled, whether the other had gained or lost weight. The amazing agility to assess these details without giving any indications of their observations came from practice. In these areas, the women were highly skilled. Most of them were friends, holding long conversations on the phone, lunching together. They shared intimate details of their lives, demanding of, and relying on the other 'not to breathe a word of it'. On the whole, in their own way they were loyal, and always supportive.

Did they betray these confidences? Yes. All the time. They managed to know everything about each other, details they swore on all things holy never to divulge. Because they were so discreet, they could whisper in others' ears, swear to absolute secrecy, and, in so doing, manage to be fully informed without any of them ever being caught.

The men were more overt, wearing their success like a badge. Assured, clever, astute and shrewd, they were accomplished conversationalists who could switch subjects without hesitation, and with insight and knowledge. Whether they'd stepped into their fathers' shoes, or had made their own way, sometimes from humble beginnings, they were without exception the cream of their society.

Medical specialists, barristers, managing directors of dynamic companies, they rated personal excellence in their daily occupations as their primary objective. They were cultured, knew classical music, recognised composers, named obscure pieces, regularly attended the theatre, could dissect a play with knowledge and intelligence. They were also extremely generous and gave substantially to worthy causes. For that reason, above all else, they were admired, respected and well regarded.

As they chose their lives, so had they chosen their wives – with foresight and planning, often guided, and approved of, by their mothers. Marriage was the most important step they would take, and although the matches were not always perfect, they were made to work. In this circle, divorce was a rare occurrence, and would be looked upon as something shameful, a failure, a fall from grace.

Even forced marriages seemed to work. Amongst these friends were two gay men, homosexuals who had never come out of the closet.

They'd married plain girls from wealthy backgrounds with whom they had children. Although they endured complicated relationships, they were well supported by empathetic family members and friends, who may have surmised their friends' sexual orientation, but never alluded to it, never breathed a word of it.

It was in this rare atmosphere that Maryssa had found herself after her marriage to Keith. She was somewhat accepted, but it hadn't been easy. These people had gone through schools together, their families had been friends from when they were young. Maryssa was from another city. She was a stranger to them. Ultimately, it was Keith who carried her forward, gave her status. His abilities made him a leading personality in the city on all levels.

He was listened to, his opinions valued and respected. He was also extremely wealthy. In this circle of wealthy people, he was by far the richest. This made the greatest impression on them. They were surprised that he'd married an 'unknown' from another city. There were many eligible young women with excellent pedigrees born and bred in Cape Town. But Keith had taken time to warm towards the idea of marriage. Although he was deemed a tough businessman, at heart he was a poet. He'd written verses about subjects that moved him – a wonderful piece about the declaration of the independence of Israel that, amongst other contributions, was published in the Jewish tableaux – strong musical lines that touched the readers. When it came to love, he knew that he needed to be moved body and soul. He wanted a wife, someone with whom he could share his life, but the women that he'd considered had left him unconvinced. Something was always missing.

A mutual friend suggested Maryssa.

When he told his best friend that he'd met her, that 'This is it!', that he would be proposing to her soon, the friend suggested that he first meet the family.

'That won't be necessary,' he'd responded. 'I'm marrying her. Not her family.'

Daniel and his wife were the last to arrive. He knew that Maryssa was there. He'd always sensed her presence before seeing her. He walked through the crowd to where she stood. He saw her bare shoulders, the auburn glints in her hair. Maryssa. His pulse quickened. His heart beat faster.

She turned and saw him. Her tawny eyes met his intense gaze. 'Daniel!' she smiled.

How beautiful she is, he thought. 'Maryssa…'

'It's nice to see you.'

He nodded, smiled and tried to answer. The impact of seeing her had a profoundly unsettling effect on him.

'It's been a long time,' she said softly. Her heart leaped as she looked deeply into his eyes. He's changed, she thought. Daniel had always had a boyishness about him. He'd been spontaneous, something of a free spirit. Now he appeared calmer, smoother, controlled and contained. She reminded herself that a long time had passed since they'd last seen each other. 'What've you been doing? Did you specialise?'

He nodded.

'In neurology? That's what you wanted, isn't it?'

'I did. But I changed my mind. I'm a cardiologist.'

'Oh…well done. Did you study in London?'

'Yes. I got back about eighteen months ago.'

'You're in practice?'

'I am. I've got rooms in the medical centre. I'm also lecturing.'

They were quiet for a few moments.

Then she said, 'I heard that you're married.'

He did not answer but his silence was a confirmation. Then, almost imperceptibly he nodded. They watched each other intently.

'She's a lawyer?'

'She is.'

'When?'

'About eight months ago.'

'Daniel…'

'Leave it, Maryssa.' His eyes darkened. 'Tell me about you. What have you been up to?'

'I did an arts degree. I majored in English and Philosophy.'

'What can you do with that?'

'I've signed up for a Masters in English. I hope to become a writer.'

'A writer?'

'Yes. I love English. I love literature. I would love to write.'

'Fiction?'

'Novels.' She smiled at him. 'Love stories.'

'Love stories? With happy endings, I hope. Will you write our story?'

'Perhaps I will…one day…'

'Not now?'

'No. Not now.'

He nodded. 'Too soon…' he said. 'Too painful… And not a happy ending…'

'Stop, Dan, please.' She turned away. Her eyes were becoming moist.

'Daniel!' A sunny voice preceded the woman who now took his arm. 'You disappeared!' She looked at Maryssa curiously and smiled. 'Hi. I'm Jill.'

'I'm Maryssa.'

'Oh. Hi. Nice to meet. You two know each other?'

'Yes,' Maryssa answered coolly.

Daniel observed her. She was now completely in charge of her emotions, quietly confident and self-assured. She became the perfectly suited wife of a wealthy and successful man.

'From way back, I suppose?' Jill turned to Daniel.

'That's right. We go back a long way.' His tone was slightly defensive.

'I see…' Jill smiled, carefully watching them.

She was a tall girl, almost as tall as Daniel, and obviously pregnant. Maryssa saw that although she was not pretty, she had a sweet smile and smooth flushed cheeks. Her honey-toned hair was done in a French knot. She looked a lot younger than Daniel.

'When's your baby due?' Maryssa smiled.

'In October…'

'Something wonderful for both of you to look forward to…'

'Yes. We're very excited.' She hung onto Daniel's arm. 'Do you have children?'

'We do. Three. Two boys and a girl.'

'Are you talking about our brood, darl?' Keith joined them.

Daniel noted that he was a tall man, strongly built, ruggedly handsome with sharp blue eyes.

He stood close to Maryssa, put his arm possessively around her shoulders, and said affectionately, 'I've been looking for you, sweetheart. Couldn't see you in the crowd…'

'My husband Keith. Meet Daniel and…' Maryssa hesitated, then, 'Jill,' and watched as they shook hands, watched the hands of both these men who knew her so intimately.

They spoke, exchanging generalities, but Maryssa was not registering. Seeing Daniel again, standing so close to him, aroused feelings in her that she'd thought were long dead and buried. She felt uneasy and conspicuous, and was grateful when others joined them, enabling her to move away without being noticed. But Daniel noticed.

For them, the evening was no longer a congenial meeting with their friends. They moved through it automatically, speaking to other guests when spoken to, smiling, nodding, pretending to sip wine. They avidly avoided making eye contact, at the same time did not want to lose sight of each other, and all the time intensely aware of how their presence churned forgotten feelings in them.

Later that evening, Maryssa noticed Daniel standing alone in a corner of the terrace. She could no longer keep away. He watched her walk towards him, saw the familiar thrust of her slender hips, her body fluid in black silk. Her heart was beating loudly, her pale face suffused with colour.

She smiled and said in her gentle voice, 'So, here we are, meeting again, but both married to other people…'

He smiled, his smile thin and faintly sardonic, as he leaned against the wall in the way he'd always leant with one foot bent inward against the other.

She asked, 'Do you remember when you told me, long ago, that I was doing the wrong thing? That I was, to quote you, "making the mistake of a lifetime" by marrying Keith?'

'I remember,' he said.

'Do you still think I did the wrong thing?'

He was no longer smiling. 'No,' he answered. 'You did nothing wrong. It was me. I did the wrong thing. I made a mistake. The mistake of a lifetime…' The expression in his eyes was intense. His face was dark with pain. He said slowly and deliberately, 'I had you. I let you go. And I lost you. That's the mistake I made. And that is what I'll have to live with for the rest of my life.'

They faced each other, separated by invisible forces. Overwhelmed by their intense feelings, they longed to hold each other, never to let go. He wanted to take her in his arms, to feel her hair brush his face, to kiss her with a consuming passion that filled every fibre of his being. He wanted to have her kiss him, to hold him, to want him as much as he wanted her.

In those moments, they knew that the love they'd had for each other all those long years ago had not in any way diminished. It remained a bright flame, fiercely burning, intense and consuming, a flame that, for them, would continue to burn forever.

Away from the rainbow lights of the crystals, the laughter and chatter of the crowd, in a corner of the terrace, immersed in shadow, he took her hand. It was as soft and small as he remembered it to be.

They gazed deeply into each other's eyes, ravenously absorbing the love that surrounded and penetrated them, and for a few rapturous moments, felt bound together as one.

Then slowly, sorrowfully, he let go of her.

Overcome with a pain that was almost physical, Maryssa turned away. Above her, the sky was a black canopy studded with stars that stretched away to the horizon.

'How dark the sea is at night,' she whispered.

She gazed for a while at the emptiness of the vast eternal space above her, at the unknown mysteries of the black ocean in the far distance, at the ghostly outlines of the whispering trees.

When she turned round, Daniel was no longer there.

www.ingramcontent.com/pod-product-compliance
Lightning Source LLC
Chambersburg PA
CBHW030212130726
47898CB00012B/994